Snowflakes and Quartz

*STORIES OF EARLY DAYS
IN THE SAN JUAN MOUNTAINS*

By
LOUIS WYMAN

ILLUSTRATED
Revised/Second Edition

Published By
Simpler Way Book Company
P.O. Box 556
Silverton, Colorado 81433

LOUIS WYMAN, author
The Wyman Collection, San Juan County Historical Society.

First Printing · April 1977
Second Printing · September 1993

© 1993 by John Marshall · All Rights Reserved
Printed in the United States of America
ISBN 0-9632028-1-2

Typesetting and design by Serai Communication Arts · Durango, Colorado
The photographs in this volume were reproduced, enhanced and printed using digital technology by Susan Ann Matthews, Serai Communication Arts.

LOUIS WYMAN, SR.
The Wyman Collection, San Juan County Historical Society.

This book is dedicated to my Father, a true San Juaner. For him, the high country never dimmed. His visions, his dreams and his adventures, he shared with me.

Louis Wyman

Snowflakes and Quartz

Revised/Second Edition

Table of Contents

Scare 1
By Appointment Only 7
A Mistake 9
Picnic 11
The First 13
Kentuck's Last Ride 27
Shenanigans 29
Clinky 33
Problem Solved 36
Johnny-Mac 39
Pay Dirt 41
Monickers 45
Winning a Monicker 47
El Rio de las Animas Perdidas 51
Harry 54
George's Bean Boiler 56
Poco Loco 59
The Sellout 63
The Schoolmarm 65
The Happening 67
Spruce Tree Soup 69
The Old Man 71
Cool, Real Cool 74
Accidents Are For Keeps 77
Polly 81
The Big Horses 85
Tommyknocker Hoistman 87
You'll Have to Tell Old Jim 89
Blockade 95
We Lost the Shovel 105
Rapid Transit 109
The Long Boards 111
Wings on the Mountain 113
They're Gone Now 116
The Petticoat Battle 119
We Hung Our Lamps on a Portal Post 121
Honky-Tonk Ghosts 125
Old Nate's Christmas Party 129
IN MEMORIAM 133

This is Waldheim, a beautiful mansion that once sat just outside Silverton, built by Ed Stoiber. Ray Doud Photo from the Jim Bell/Gerald Glanville Collection.

Scare

In my neighborhood, when I was young, there were several families with boys about my age, give or take a year or two, all of us working hard to break loose from our mothers' apron strings. The few years before you become a teenager are dangerously wild and exciting. Things happen to you, and they catch you unawares. There's nobody around to help, so you go it alone and somehow live to tell how it happened.

If ever a place was created just for a gang of growing boys, my home town was it. The old-timers built it down in a small valley, and there wasn't much room left for it to grow. Four great mountains hemmed it in, one on each quadrant of the compass. From their peaks high above timberline, they sloped down steeply through spruce forests to the very fence posts of our back yards. For the boys in my gang, those mountains held a challenge that couldn't be ignored. The Wizard of Oz fairy land of adventure.

Anvil Mountain, on the west side of town, was the closest and lowest. It was our mountain. We conquered it. We took it by conquest and defended that huge pile of rock against all comers. The rustlers we hanged to our hangin' tree, and the Indian war parties we drove from its peak would make the Lone Ranger and old General Custer shiver in their boots.

In the valleys and canyons between the mountains abandoned mining operations were falling into ruins. King Silver had been dethroned and had gone elsewhere. An industry was struggling to adjust. There were two old smelters, several mills, a brewery that turned out nothing but rats and mice, and cabins built by prospectors tucked away in hidden gulches on mountain sides. These relics of better times invited us to explore, and we never turned down an invitation.

One beautiful summer morning, Pinky, Jimmy, and I launched an expedition into "Enemy Territory" as we called it whenever we left our stronghold on Anvil Mountain. We were headed for Arrastra Gulch, a tributary that drained into the Animas Canyon from the east. On our way we had to pass the old Silver Lake mill and Waldheim, a huge red brick mansion Ed Stoiber built when he owned and operated the Silver Lake Mine.

We had to hike up the railroad track on the west side of the river. Waldheim was built on a small flat piece of land on the east side. That immense pile of brick and stone, to us, was the greatest challenge of all, to somehow find a way to get into the mansion just to see what it had been like and what had happened to it through the years of idleness. But there wasn't a chance. The east side of the river was off limits. The company that owned the property at that time kept a watchman or caretaker to look after the mill and Waldheim. His name was Joe Hinkley. He lived in a neat little company house there beside the tracks where he could see most everything that happened from his front porch.

1

So we climbed up into Arrastra Basin, on the chance we might pick up some junk copper and make a dime or two. But that didn't work out either. A crew of mill-hands was repairing the equipment, getting ready for a start up. They wouldn't let us hang around because, they said, "You might get hurt." That was stupid. They were the ones that got hurt. We never did. Oh, maybe a bloody nose, a few cut fingers, and a black eye now and then. But those men who worked in the mills and mines did. They got broken bones, and sometimes they were killed. A kid bounces. He's not apt to break. If kids did break easily, there wouldn't be many around to grow up.

Our expedition had become a flop. So we decided to go home. On our way we had to pass through some small parks and glades on the north side of Arrastra Gulch just before it breaks off into the Animas Canyon. A pleasant place to spend an idle hour or two. The Silver Lake Co. had built a large wooden flume four or five feet wide and about that deep, to carry water from the Animas River to a hydro-electric power plant near the mill. It spanned Arrastra Gulch and the creek at right angles on a high wooden trestle. Loitering along we looked the flume over to see if there was a chance to have some fun with it.

Pinky, who didn't like to climb unless he had to, said, "We can get inside this thing. There's no water in it and never will be any more."

"What you want'a get in there for?" Jimmy wanted to know.

"Well," Pink said, "Let's get in and go across the trestle to the other side of the gulch by walkin' along inside the flume. Then we can follow it and see what happened to the water at the flume's end. It had to go some place. And we won't have to climb in and out of that deep gulch."

At about half way across, we looked over the side to see how high we were.

"Hey, you guys!" Jimmy yelled. "Let's go back, I'm scared."

Jimmy was always getting scared. He loved it. If a day passed without a good scare, it was a day lost. His scares never interfered with the action.

We decided it was as bad to go back as to go on and began to move along slowly.

Then it happened. Pinky was the heavyweight. His feet went through the rotten flume bottom. But he saved himself by grabbing the top edge of the flume and then pulling his feet back from the hole. There we were, all three of us too scared to move. There was nothing under the rotten bottom boards but sixty or more feet of open space to the rocks below.

"I told you guys we should'a gone back," Jimmy said.

Pink was scared bad and trying not to show it. "I'm not going back. If we move along slow and hold on to the top edge like I did to keep from falling through, we can make it."

We worked it out that way. By moving very carefully and keeping ten or more feet of space between us, we arrived where the side of Arrastra Gulch came up to meet the bottom of the flume. It was real nice to be on solid ground again.

Working our way from there to the end was just routine exploration. The thing ended abruptly in a large square tank. A big steel pipe took the water on down to a turbine in a powerhouse. But the big surprise was when we looked over the tank's edge to see where we were, right there below us was the Waldheim Mansion. Our expedition had suddenly become exciting. As Jimmy said, "I could throw a rock right out there on the roof."

"Better not, Jimmy," I said. "The old man might be around somewheres, and he'd hear it and start lookin'."

As usual, Pinky came up with a suggestion to get things moving again.

"Listen, you guys. Two of us could stay up here and keep watch, while one guy slipped down to see if any of those windows in the basement are unlocked, so we could open it. We'll draw straws to see who goes. Maybe we'll get to see what's inside that old place yet."

Jimmy pulled the short straw. "OK, you guys. If I look up here and don't see you, I'll know you've cut out, and I'll go too. Stay in sight so I can see you. OK?"

He went over the tank side like a cat. To breach the walls of that mammoth old red brick citadel, and explore it from dungeon to roof, would be the very acme of adventure.

We couldn't have selected a better man for the job. Jimmy slipped down the hill, keeping low in the brush, until he reached level ground that might have been a lawn at one time. From there to the side of the mansion he had no cover. He looked up and saw both of us watching, then went like a scared rabbit to the nearest window. He worked at it for a few minutes, but it was tight. He looked up again, saw Pink and me still on sentry duty, and moved to the next window. It seemed to me he'd hardly touched it, and it opened. Jimmy dived through! He was inside the Mansion!

Like Jimmy, we went over the tank's side, down the hill, and through the window. Pink and I were not going to let Jimmy have all the fun going through the old building while we stood up there in a water tank like a couple of frogs in a barrel. Jimmy was sitting on a flight of stairs waiting for us. The first thing he said was, "I'm scared."

"Listen, you guys." Pink had more on his mind than musty old mansions.

"I'm either going through that door up there or out the window again. The way this cellar stinks it's full of rats, and I don't like rats."

The door at the top of the stairs opened easily, and we stepped through it into what must have been a kitchen. A great hotel-type coal range stood against one wall. There was a rough wooden table with a rack nailed up overhead for the cook to hang his pots and pans on, and a sink built of planks about ten feet long with a drain hole in one end fitted with a round plug and a cold water tap in the other end.

"Not much of a kitchen for a mansion," Pink said.

Another doorway opened from the kitchen to a smaller room which had been the butler's pantry. There were lots of shelves and bins, but little else. A third opening had no door. Just beyond it stood a large screen, and you had to walk around it to get into the room beyond. We did, and found that we were in the dining room. Simply by stepping from behind the screen, as if by magic, the whole character of the building changed.

Every place you looked there was oak. Oak floors, oak wainscoting, oak paneling, the door and window casings were all of solid oak, dirty, smudged and marred. But the room still told you what it once had been.

We stood in one place and turned around a time or two, just looking.

"Gee, you guys! Ain't you scared?" Jimmy wanted to know.

I think all three of us were a bit overwhelmed by the way our prank was turning out. But stopping now was out of the question. We were inside the famous Waldheim Mansion, a dream coming true. We passed from the dining room into a great hall where stairs led to the floor above. That massive sweep of oak steps and banisters was a little more than we could handle right then. So we moved on toward the front of the building to a large room that had been an office. Someone had blasted the steel door from a vault. The door lay face down with all that locking mechanism exposed. It kind of made your stomach turn over. The place was a litter of papers and trash, nothing that could interest us. And we went back to the great hall to face the massive oak staircase again.

Climbing that thing was going to separate the timid from the bold. We had no idea what we'd find up there.

"Gee whiz," Jimmy said. "We gonna climb up?"

Pink and I were just as scared as Jimmy, but we'd never admit it. Jimmy was the only one who had that privilege. He never let it interfere with the action. He was the first to put a foot on the bottom step.

Our expedition almost bogged down on a landing midway between floors, where the stairs swept around on an angle up to the second floor. It was kind of dark up there, but we could see light at the end of the stairway. So we moved up slowly and finally got to where we could peek over the top step and see if we should run or stay.

A long hall extended to a window in a far wall. Several doors opened off on either side. Most of the doors we tried were locked. Finally I tried one that opened. The room was a bedroom, much of its furniture still in place, every piece solid Bird's-eye maple. Years later I learned that Captain Jack (Mrs. Stoiber) had furnished each bedroom with a different kind of wood. It would be hard to imagine, but we had a hint of what the Mansion at Waldheim was like when the Stoibers lived there.

Exploring that floor didn't take too long. We could get into only a few rooms. Then we found another flight of stairs, not nearly so impressive as the main ones. This flight went straight up to the floor above with only a short landing about half way up. We could see the top, and it was well lighted up there. Slowly, so as not to get ourselves into something we couldn't handle, we climbed. At the top we came out into what must have been the mansion's ballroom. A large room was built in the space usually used as an attic. The walls which were not high had dormer windows on all four sides. Upholstered seats were fastened to the walls between the windows and an arched ceiling reached high overhead. A beautiful room, light and pleasant and still fairly clean.

What made us gape was a full sized pool table right there in the center of what was once a beautiful dance floor, with a set of pool balls all racked and ready for a game. A case fastened to the wall between two windows held a dozen cues. We couldn't understand why a pool table was set up in the middle of a ballroom. And I've never found out since. But each of us grabbed a cue, and the game was on. More shooting than scoring.

Every now and then, Jimmy ran over to a lookout window on the west from which he could see the watchman's house. Jimmy was to warn us if he saw old Joe coming, so we could make our getaway before Hinkley could get to the mansion's front door. The last trip Jimmy made, he came running back to the table.

"Be quiet, you guys," he hissed. "That man Hinkley is right down there in front of the mansion. He'll be coming up the porch steps and in the front door in just a minute. He's gonna catch us, and maybe we'll all have to go to jail. What are we gonna do?"

There didn't seem to be anything we could do. Our only out was down the stairs, and old Joe was down there. If we went out on the roof and tried to drop to the ground, we'd get hurt seriously.

"Listen, you guys." Pinky was putting a stunt together again. "If we could scare the old man bad enough, so he'd run home for help, we'd have time to get away."

"How you gonna scare him?" Jimmy and I wanted to know.

We were ready to try anything that might work. The predicament we were in could get painful.

"Get those pool balls over to the stairs quick," he said. "Now line 'em up on the top step. Good. Now when we hear the door open, shove 'em all down the stairs at once. Make 'em bounce high!"

In a matter of seconds we had the pool balls lined up and ready. Just in time. We heard the front door hinges squeak.

Fifteen big, hard pool table balls, with the cue ball thrown in for good measure, cascaded down a flight of bare oak stair treads, all at the same time and bouncing high. They must have sounded to poor old Hinkley like the whole Mansion was tumbling down on his head. The racket was deafening. I hurried over to our lookout window to see if Pink's stunt was doing us any good. The pool balls had done their work well. The old man was not particularly athletic, but he was running fast and clawing at the air with both hands for more speed.

"OK, you guys, beat it. He's running for home as fast as he can go!"

We went too, racing down the stairs, through the kitchen into the cellar, and out the window. Then we ran for our lives up into the heavy spruce forest on the mountain side. We never stopped until we had to rest. All of us flopped down in a little grassy spot. Pinky never moved after he hit the ground, and I wasn't much better off. But that guy Jimmy was stretched out comfortably on his back in a small patch of sunshine. He had his cap bill pulled down to shade his eyes, and his hands were laced behind his head for a pillow.

Suddenly he started to laugh. "Gee whiz, you guys," he said. "That was the best scare we ever had! Let's go home."

Silverton school finery. The group photograph was taken in front of the Silverton Public School, June, 1893. San Juan County Historical Society.

A couple of kids look in on a real barbershop located on Greene Street. San Juan County Historical Society.

By Appointment Only

By the time I was old enough to run around the neighborhood and play ball with the other kids, my father had sold out his freighting business and could spend a lot of time at home with the family.

Dad was a true San Juaner. He made his money in the San Juan, and he spent it there. Never once did he lose faith in the mines, the town or the Colorado High Country. He had amazing physical strength and ambition and dreams to match it. Once he decided on a course of action, right or wrong, he followed it to the end. If people or things got in his way, he brushed them aside and plowed on. Remembering some of the things he did still brings a laugh, even when he warmed up my personal "Hot Line" that ran from the seat of my pants to the region between my ears. Life with the Old Gent was a never-ending adventure, filled with all the excitement and fun any kid could ask for.

He was a great advocate of physical culture and the manly art of self-defense. A set of kid's boxing gloves arrived via parcel post one day. That summer the neighborhood kids punched and hammered on each other until their mamas put a stop to it. But we sure learned to throw a punch and duck one. Something every kid should know.

Father's habit of doing what he wanted without a thought as to how the results would affect other people was responsible for some pretty hectic situations. We kids loved it. Whatever he was doing, we'd rally around, knowing we'd get a part of the action.

One of his pet theories was that a boy should have his hair shingled in the springtime as soon as the warm weather came round. Each spring he'd get out a pair of old hair clippers and we'd retire to the barn's carriage room for a little hair cutting. One of my friends from across the street always took advantage of a chance for a free haircut, and his maw was grateful too. Usually our gang was on hand to witness the ritual of shingling a boy's hair, and of course my pal and I were the envy of everyone.

Some of the others needed haircuts too. They always did, no doubt about that. And it was decided that any one who didn't have his hair shingled that summer was a "so and so." They lined up according to their importance in the gang, and Dad went to work with his clippers. It didn't make a particle of difference to him if the kid's parents approved or not. As far as he was concerned, it was good for us youngsters. So we spent the afternoon getting our heads clipped right down to the skin.

When all the haircuts were finished up to everyone's satisfaction, the kids ran home to show their mothers the latest hair style. For some reason, mothers love golden locks of hair, auburn curls or a nice straight part on one side of a young gentleman's head to enhance his childish masculinity. It must have been a shock to those poor mothers to discover what a knob-headed, bat-eared imp had been hidden under those beautiful mops of hair.

The neighborhood exploded. Women were running back and forth from house to house, dragging bristly-headed kids after them. One mother was screaming over her back fence while she held up her darling eight-year-old baby boy who had been scalped by that awful Mr. Wyman. It was more exciting than a Fourth of July celebration. They made a lot of noise for awhile, but after a time they went inside, and the place quieted down.

Then the telephone started to ring. Dad answered the first two calls. He hung up on the last one and gave orders that no one was to answer the phone. He stamped out to the barn in a huff. That evening, some of the neighborhood fathers sent word: They could handle their own family affairs, including haircuts, and would he please leave their kids alone.

Next day nobody showed up to play, so I went to see where everybody was. I found out not one could come over and play in my yard any more, and I was told not to come and play in theirs either. But the vacant lots where we had our ball diamond was neutral ground. By mid-afternoon we were all there, really excited about the reaction our haircuts had caused.

Some of the guys said their dads could lick mine, and they were going to do it. I told them my dad could lick any two of theirs with one of his hands tied behind his back. Thinking about it now, I still think he could. Some said their mothers were going to take my old man to court and sue for damages—maybe millions of dollars.

That scared me a little and I ran home to find out what it meant. Dad said there was nothing to it, and to go on back and play with the kids. So I told him the other kids' dads were going to give him a good licking.

"Well," he said, "I guess I'll have to be there when they do." The grin on his face gave me all the assurance I needed.

For a few days we were so busy watching for the fights to start, we didn't have much time for play. We watched like hawks. To have missed anything would have been worse than taking a licking ourselves. The only thing that happened was the kids' mothers glaring at Dad from their front porches when he went down the street.

The gang enjoyed the hassle and excitement, and the best thing about it was, we didn't have to comb our hair all summer.

A Mistake

Nobody knows more about a small town—its streets, alleys, boarded-up buildings and what goes on behind closed doors—than the kids who live there.

My cousin Bud and I were as wise as any of our gang. By the time I was ten and he was twelve, we knew our town inside out and were branching out into the surrounding countryside for greater fields of exploration.

Old industrial plants of any kind offer a world of excitement and challenge to a small boy. Our big interest at that moment was an abandoned smelter a half-mile or so south of town. It held vast possibilities for bold young adventurers. Dilapidated stairways with missing treads and banisters were scary and led to unknown dangers in the tower cell far above. A boy's imagination can turn rusting machinery and worthless junk into engines of destruction more fantastic than a Jules Verne creation. But most exciting of all was taking a dare to scout out the spine-tingling dark places where pack rats lurked, and your life depended on the deadly accuracy of a sling-shot pellet. Only the valiant could subdue those gargantuan beasts of prey.

But the make-believe day of a ten or twelve-year-old must, like all days, come to an end. The sun dropping down toward Sultan Mountain's ridge in the west seemed to say: "You kids aren't big enough to be out alone after dark. It's time you went home."

For young adventurers who have campaigned in strange lands, the road home is always a long and wearisome journey. For Bud and me, it promised to be very long indeed on that warm August afternoon.

Good luck suddenly came our way as we trudged homeward through the dusk. A team of high-stepping bays hitched to a handsome surrey came along and pulled up alongside us. It was one of those fancy rigs livery stables kept for special customers or occasions. The rubber-tired wheels and chassis were enameled a brilliant canary yellow. A black leather dashboard matched the leather mudguards, and the top was as elegant as the rest of the vehicle.

Four fashionably dressed women smiled down on us and asked if we'd like to ride into town with them. For a few seconds, we hesitated, but Bud spotted a big box of chocolates on one lady's lap, and it was more than he could resist. He scrambled up into the front seat. I wasn't going to be left to walk home by myself. So I climbed up into the back seat with the help of a welcoming hand.

They were beautifully gowned ladies, with lace and ruffles everywhere. The feathers in their great hats almost touched the surrey's top. The lady who drove wore tight black gloves reaching to her elbows. I wondered how she ever got 'em on and off. Their perfume even overcame the horse smell as we drove along. It was wonderful.

Bud and I had found a bonanza. He sat between the two in the front seat, and I between the two women on the back seat. Each of us had one hand deep in a box of chocolates, and a bottle of strawberry soda pop gripped in the other. And our pockets were full of chewing gum and lemon drops. There were some tall bottles of julep in a hamper we thought we'd like to try. But julep was a lady's drink; young men didn't use it. The world had never been so fine, or so much fun.

The fact that the ladies in the front seat were proprietors of The Bon Ton and The Arcade dance halls made no difference to either of us. The dusky lady on my right, who held forth at The Ethiopian Temple of Pleasure (as the local gentry dubbed her establishment), was as kindly and jolly as could be. In no time at all, the bays had whisked us into town. Our hostesses wanted to know where we lived. We told them in the north end. Nobody has ever used street names and numbers in Silverton—you just go where you want to go. They said they'd drive up Greene Street and let us out in front of the Town Hall, and we could run home from there. Two kids never rode up their home town main street in grander style.

We didn't make it all the way to the Town Hall. Dad was standing on the sidewalk in front of the Post Office, and it seemed to me he took only two steps before he reached the surrey and yanked us out by the collars. How he could whop both our butts and head us up the street toward home at the same time, I'll never know. But he did.

When Dad came home that evening, I thought there was a twinkle in his eyes, but his mouth was as grim as a night cop's on Saturday night. He never said a word to Mother, or anyone else, about what had happened. I was glad of that, because by bed time, my belly wasn't feeling too good. Mother took my temperature, and it was normal. I thought that was the end of it, and tried to sneak off to bed. But it didn't work.

There is nothing in this world that can ruin a kid's day like castor oil.

Look closely—can you see the four ladies? The picture was taken in 1951 near Red Mountain Lodge but does not indicate the age of the surrey. Dyson McNaughton Collection, San Juan County Historical Society.

Picnic

July and August are the picnic months, a custom practiced by most communities. The modes of their celebrations change with time, but usually each has a procedure that is uniquely their own.

One of Silverton's more lovable citizens was the Colonel, a son of "The Old Sod", a bachelor, and a gentleman of means. It was his habit to indulge his whims lavishly, and he loved the limelight. Each year, he chartered a special train to transport the Sunday school kids on a picnic at Maggie Gulch, eight miles north of town. The fact that the Sunday school classes suddenly tripled or quadrupled on picnic day never troubled the Colonel at all. The train, ice cream cones and soda pop was free to all who came, and all were welcome. Influential members of the church helped out with watermelons and various other necessities to round out a day for the kids.

Railroad accommodations consisted of a combination baggage car and coach, and whatever freight car happened to be available. Often the train was made up with just the coach and a gondola car, and the picnic crowd would climb aboard at the old D&RG depot.

Departure time at 10:00 a.m. sharp could never be achieved, getting people aboard a train with all their picnic goodies just can't be done in a hurry, even with the Colonel expediting the loading. Invariably, after making a start, they'd have to stop and back up for a straggler or two.

Of course little tots and their mothers rode in the coach with the deacons, committee members and their host. All picnic supplies were stuffed into the baggage compartment, leaving the gondola free for kids, their teachers and the overflow from the coach. If there's anything with greater potential for chaos than a railroad gondola full of kids, I've not heard of it.

By the time the special reached Howardsville, half of them had cinders in their eyes, and some small ones who couldn't see over the car sides wanted to be held up so they could. And the rest wanted to go to the toilet. (We didn't use the term bathroom then; few people had one. A number three washtub in front of the kitchen stove on Saturday night, and a privy out back was about it.) But, I digress.

Lunch boxes that had been carefully placed on the floor along the gondola's sides became vulnerable, too. They simply couldn't withstand the battering of kids stumbling over them, and leaking pickle juice bore mute evidence of a mess inside.

Somehow these dedicated souls, the teachers, managed to hold their charges together until they arrived at the picnic grounds. And the Colonel's picnic was off to a good start with hours of fun ahead for everyone. Kids raced, played games, and contested for prizes provided by the Colonel. A silver dollar could bring a Herculean effort from the small contestants. Then the action slipped away, as if by magic. Every mouth was filled with eats, ice cream cones, soda pop, cake, pickles and sandwiches until they could eat no more.

By the time the conductor tooted all aboard for town, things had slowed down to a crawl. The return trip wasn't like the run up the canyon; a little whimpering and crying replaced the laughter and shouting of the morning. Along with the cinders, a few bellyaches had to be eased, some bruises and cuts bandaged, and a little one consoled for her hat which blew away and fell in the river. And sunburn was everybody's problem. The elders' bright smiles had changed to frowns of annoyance, and the smart habits of the ladies suffered in like degree. But they brought the day's campaign to a successful end like true veterans.

There's an old hymn that goes something like this:

> *Will there be any stars in my crown*
> *When at evening the sun goeth down?*

I think the psalmist must have had Sunday school teachers and kindly old Colonels in mind when he wrote it.

The First

Dad's daydreams were not the idle musings or the fantasies of a mystic. They had a way of erupting into reality. After one had run its course, nothing in the vicinity was ever the same. His tremendous physical drive and capacity for brushing obstacles aside made him both envied and respected. By the time I was ten years old he was cutting me in for as much of the action as I could handle.

He advocated and built good roads. The summer of 1910 he was up to his sweatband in a project that took in half the State of Colorado. He envisioned an automobile highway, unheard of at the time, running southwest from Denver through the scenic grandeur of the High Colorado Rockies. The road would traverse a thousand miles or more of the state's finest recreational land, finally circling back to Denver. Years later, when all the county roads had been connected, it became known as "Colorado's Thousand Mile Circle Route." Of course Silverton and The San Juan were bright stars along the way.

To publicize his dream Dad enlisted the help of a lifelong friend, Dr. D. L. Mechling, an automobile buff of Denver. Although no relation, he was Uncle Mech to the Wyman family. Mechling and Dad had shared the same beanpot and campfire for several years while they gathered a few dollars together so they could set themselves up in business. Dad stayed in The San Juan. The Doctor hung his shingle up in Denver. Their mutual friendship and trust never dimmed.

About the first of July that year, Uncle Mech's son Tug (Eugene) arrived in Silverton on the evening train. Tug was trying to throw off the effects of a hard go with typhoid fever! Uncle Mech, knowing the Wymans would be in camp on the Rio Grand River all summer, sent him down to be with us until fall, thinking the outdoor life and Mother's cooking would bring his health back to normal. Dad and I met him at the depot. Dad of course knew Tug, having visited many times in the Mechling home. But I'd never seen him before. The slim kid, a head taller than me, who stepped down from the chaircar vestibule didn't look too promising a companion for a summer in camp. But wonder of wonders, under his arm he carried a rifle scabbard with a shiny stock glinting from the open end of it. My evaluation of Tug took a sharp rise.

After the greetings were over and Tug had answered all of Dad's questions, I finally got in a word.

"That your gun?"

"That's right, and I have plenty of ammunition too."

"What make is it?"

"It's a Winchester bolt-action .22. My father had a new-type Lyman peep sight put on it for me."

"Gee, maybe you'll let me shoot it once in a while?"

"Sure, if your father says it's all right. Don't you have a gun?"

"Nope. I'm gonna get one on my twelfth birthday."

A good rifle or sidearm is often the catalyst for cementing a lifelong friendship. For two boys about to spend the summer in camp, how could it miss? Throughout the following weeks Tug, his rifle, and I were inseparable.

During the previous winter Dad and Uncle Mech had made plans that called for Tug's father to drive his car southwest from Denver to Colorado Springs, Pueblo, and on to Creede, Colorado. From there he'd make his way up the Rio Grande River Valley as best he could to Camp Wyman, where we'd be in camp waiting for him. He was to time his departure from Denver so as to arrive at camp about the last of August. Then Dad, Tug and I would join him in an attempt to drive the car over the Continental Divide at Stoney Pass and on into Silverton. If an automobile was able to negotiate that 12, 500 foot mountain barrier it would prove automobile highways to the Western Slope were feasible over any mountain pass in the state.

Our summer's outing was off to a good start. Within a fortnight after Tug's arrival in Silverton a small mountain of camping paraphernalia had been assembled—all the equipment two families and several guests would need for a summer in camp. Then for two days we trekked by packtrain, saddlehorses and a three-seated covered rig with a four horse hitch to transport the women and kids up over the Continental Divide at Stoney Pass. Once through the gap we followed the Rio Grande River from its headwaters down to our permanent camp site, where the rendezvous with Uncle Mech and his automobile would take place late in August.

The weatherman had been in a kindly mood all summer. He seemed reluctant to unwrap September and fold away the last days of August. He'd found a glorious masterpiece of nature's beauty in each one of them. For two youngsters they were golden days filled with fishing poles, fighting trout, hotcakes floating in syrup, gun oil and a .22 rifle together with all the ammunition and freedom we could use.

Lookout Point at Camp Wyman became a staging area for Tug and me. A place to rest from our last exploit and plan another. Scanning the upper valley, that portion visible from the Point, became a ritual we repeated many times as the last of August drew near. The old ones—the Indians who came there first as lookouts while they chipped away at their flint arrowheads—never kept a keener watch over the valley below than we did. Even the flint chips and bits of broken arrows sifted through our fingers almost unnoticed. Breaking the news that Uncle Mech had arrived would be the most exciting bit of action of the summer so far.

At the breakfast table one morning Dad said, "This is the last day of August. Mech should show up today with the car, if he hasn't run into trouble."

That was enough for Tug and me. We stuffed our pockets with apples and cookies left from yesterday's baking and raced out to take up our watch at the Point.

"If Uncle Mech don't get here by dark—I wonder if Dad will saddle up in the morning and ride out to see what happened. Maybe we can go with him?"

Tug's faith in his father never wavered. "He'll be here, Lew. Watch and see."

All at once Tug stiffened to attention again. "Did you hear that Lew?"

"Yea. What is it?"

We both bounded to our feet. The deep throbbing voice of a big bore gasoline engine rose on the warm air from somewhere below us—a sound never heard in the valley before. There was an automobile down there someplace working its way along two wagonwheel ruts that answered for a road.

"He made it. It's here!" Tug's shout was half-scream. "The car's gotta show somewhere down in one of them parks. Lew, watch every one."

"Sure I am. What color is it?"

"Red."

A few minutes later, in one of the meadows perhaps a half-mile from the point, a big red automobile rolled slowly out from behind a fringe of trees and brush that had hidden it from view.

"There he is! That's my Dad down there driving our car."

He snatched up the rifle and fired a shot into the air, announcing the arrival. Then we headed for camp, throttles wide open.

Mother was waiting for us with a pan of soapsuds and two clean shirts. Having to stop long enough to scrub up at a time like this was worse than having the biggest Fourth of July skyrocket in the world fizzle out.

"I'll not have Uncle Mech and his party find you boys looking like a pair of coyote pups. Now hurry it up and don't forget to scrub behind your ears. A little extra rubbing will do some good there too."

There was no way around Mother. So Tug and I went to work with more speed than efficiency.

Somehow we survived the clean shirt and washbasin detour, making it down to the river bank just as Dad finished pulling on his hip-boots. The car would have to remain on the opposite side of the river from camp. There was no natural ford or bridge, only a fairly shallow riffle where a man in hip-boots could wade across. Since it was too deep and swift for Tug and me, we climbed up on Dad's shoulders, one on each side, and he ferried us over. We came ashore at the exact moment that the automobile crashed through a clump of willows, stopping not fifty feet from the river bank. Perfect timing.

Two men stepped down from the front seat, Tug's father and J.A. McGuire, editor of The Outdoor Life Magazine (published in Denver at that time). It would be hard to find two men less alike. Uncle Mech was as big and robust as my Dad and about the same age. Mr. McGuire was small, thin and wiry. He seemed to pop around from place to place. I don't think I ever remember seeing him move slowly. Before long, Tug and I learned he was all man, too. McGuire had joined the expedition sensing a possible story for his magazine.

"Hello, Dad!" Tug called and went scrambling up the river bank to meet his father.

They shook hands. The Doctor's searching eyes found everything he'd hoped to find in the boy he'd sent to the high country two short months before. His son was well, tough and strong as a rawhide boot lace.

Uncle Mech turned to greet Dad. They shook hands. Neither spoke for a few seconds, but there was something in their eyes that said an awful lot. Finally, when the

All chained up and headed for the top of Stoney Pass. Soon Silverton will witness the arrival of its very first automobile. The Wyman Collection, San Juan County Historical Society.

Doctor did speak, all he said was, "Thanks, Louie." Then he turned to introduce Mr. McGuire.

I think I grew up just a bit at that meeting. I realized kissing was the greeting for women and girls, men shook hands. Right then I was ready to be a man on any terms.

"Come on Lew, I'll show you the car. It's a Croxton-Keeton."

"Gee whiz, Tug. What's a Croxton-Keeton?"

"That's the name of the car and the company that makes it."

Now a word as to the car from Mr. McGuire's story published in The Outdoor Life Magazine: "It was of the Croxton-Keeton type, 30 horsepower (and it had it all too). Four cylinders—4½ inch bore, 4½ inch stroke—a car patterned almost exactly after the French Renault. Aside from the fact the water boils rather easily, the car is the acme of perfection for mountain roads."

In less than five minutes I'd been around and under the machine several times. I'd learned the size of the tires and the air pressure they required, the engine horsepower, how the new style automatic electric headlights worked, and wound up in the driver's seat with both hands clamped to the steering wheel.

Boy, oh boy, if I could just start the motor, I knew I could drive this car. No chance of that, the engine had to be cranked by hand to start it. That took a good strong arm.

For a few days our expedition was stalled at Camp Wyman. Road crews up on the pass were working long hours each day trying to get the old trail opened up so an automobile might get through. Dad was up there with them most of the time, pushing the work as hard as he could. After the first of September the pass often became snowbound until the following spring. Time for getting the car over the hump had about run out.

Dad came back to camp late one afternoon in the three-seated rig. We saw it coming down the valley, and knew in a day or two we'd break camp. Everybody got busy packing duffel bags for the trip home over the pass. The ladies and small fry would ride in the rig while their menfolk accompanied them on horseback. The ladies would make the trip home in ease, riding with a skinner Dad trusted to do the driving for them. But Tug and I wanted no part of that. We nagged, pestered, and begged our Dads to let us ride with them when they made the attempt to cross the Continental Divide by automobile. Finally in desperation to be rid of our constant yapping they gave their consent. Tug and I strutted about camp like a couple of game cocks. We were to ride with the men in the car. We had ridden with the women and girls for the last time. Getting the machine over the hill, as we called it, 25 miles in one day, was going to be a task where brute strength in men and machine would be taxed to the limit. To have womenfolk with us was out of the question.

We broke camp early, the day after the womenfolk and our guests had pulled out for home. A packtrain had arrived from Silverton to pick up the camping gear. Dad ferried Tug and me across the river for the last time. I waited breathlessly, hardly able to believe I'd be told to climb in when Uncle Mech gave the word to start.

He made a quick inspection of the car. "I guess we're ready. Turn her over J. A., and let's get on the road."

The way Mr. McGuire turned that motor over I knew, although he was small, he was all man. He had to be to travel with Dad and Uncle Mech. After a sputter or two the motor caught, settling to a steady rhythm. We were off. For a kid used to horses, teams, and wagons, the power driven machine was a "Wizard of Oz" creation. Of course Uncle Mech was driving. Dad rode on the front seat beside him, while Mr. McGuire and his camera rode in the tonneau with Tug and me.

Uncle Mech turned the car around, heading back through the willows and brush to the wagonwheel ruts. It was a heady experience for me as the machine cuffed willow branches aside or literally folded whole clumps down to the ground and passed right over them. Once out on the trail we drove along slowly. Large rocks hidden between the ruts had to be avoided. I learned—with all its power and weight—the automobile had a tender belly which had to be protected.

About a half mile up the trail from camp we came to our first real obstacle—The Rio Grand River. It swept east then west in a Great Oxbow bend at right angles to the valley. There was no way around it. The road cut straight across both channels and wound up on the same side of the river. The fords were wide and shallow, but the possibility of quicksand or a muddy bottom was a threat we couldn't ignore.

We stopped. Uncle Mech and Dad wore hip-boots in anticipation of the crossings. They waded back and forth across the river several times before they decided it was safe to try the ford with the car.

All of us piled back in again except Mr. McGuire. He moved out into the water to snap pictures of the action. Tug's dad eased the machine down the river bank until the front wheels were deep in the water. He pulled the throttle open and in we went, surging and plunging, toward the opposite bank. Water sprayed out from the front fenders in two great fans. Before I could get a second breath, we stormed up the other bank. We'd made it! Uncle Mech didn't stop or slow down. He drove right on across the neck of land and, without hesitation, plowed into the second ford. We came through that one too up onto dry land with Tug and me cheering wildly.

But our elation was short lived. Water had shorted out the distributor.

"Gee Tug, won't the car run any more? Are we stuck for good?"

"Naw, we've had it happen before. Dad'll have it fixed in a little while."

The car standing with the hood up, looked like some prehistoric beetle trying to swallow a man whole. Uncle Mech's backside and legs were all of him that was visible as he worked on the motor.

It didn't take long to get the engine feeling better. We loaded up, then headed for the north end of the valley where our grueling climb to the Continental Divide began. Our confidence was high. If the Rio Grand River couldn't stop us, nothing could. Dad and Uncle Mech shed their rubber boots for more comfortable footwear, and we settled back to enjoy the ride.

The next few miles were fairly easy. We had to stop now and then to roll away rocks that seemed too high for the car to clear. Several larger ones we had to dig out. There was no way to get by on either side. Every precaution had to be taken to protect the under carriage, rip that apart, and we'd be through for good. Before noon we pulled into Bruster's Park at the foot of Timber Hill.

This is hallowed ground. Eleven men of Captain Fremont's party froze or starved to death here in the winter of 1848-49. Old Bill Williams, Fremont's guide, had lost his way. He missed the Little Weminuche Pass and then, in the dead of winter, tried to bull

This is Silverton Pass on the Continental Divide, 12,000 feet above sea level. The picture was taken by Louis on a fishing trip to Emerald Lake. Louis Wyman Collection.

his way through the mountains to the western slope. Fremont gave up and went back for supplies, leaving eleven men camped here in the park. Tug and I searched around under trees and bushes thinking we might find some human skulls or bones. That's the way the army troops found them—so the story goes—all mixed up with skeletons of packmules the men had eaten.

From Bruster's Park to the top of Timber Hill is no great distance, but the old wagon trail is steep and narrow, covered with razor sharp trap rock. One thing was for sure, that old trail would test the car's hill-climbing ability. As Mr. McGuire said in his story. "The engine was rated at thirty horsepower, and it had every one of them too." We'd know in a short time if that horsepower was enough to get us up over the top.

"I think we're ready now," Uncle Mech said. "When we hit the steep grades I'm not going to stop or slow down if I can help it. Should the car stall out in that loose rock, it may be hard to get going again. So sit tight and I'll try and make the top on the first try."

The car lunged, bounced and bucked its way up the hill with all of us hanging on to anything we could to keep our seats. Suddenly a rear tire blew out. A stick of dynamite couldn't have made a louder bang. I thought the car was going to turn over. Tug and I hopped to the ground like squirrels. We were too excited to be scared.

Replacing the ruined casing had to be done with the wheel still mounted on the axle. First, because of the steep grade, all the wheels except the one with the flat tire had to be blocked with large rocks. When Mr. McGuire and Uncle Mech had the axle jacked up high enough, Dad slid a good-sized log under it, then blocked the log up so the car weight would rest on that instead of the jack, making it safe to work on the wheel. In time the old tire was exchanged for a new one. Then came the pleasure of pumping it up. Ninety pounds of air pressure takes a lot of pumping. All of us took turns until the pressure gauge read the required poundage. Toward the last neither Tug nor I could force the pump piston down against the pressure. Uncle Mech said we should fill our pockets with rocks for more weight. Tug and I were glad to back off. Pumping up the tire had become hard work.

"Lew, let's hang the old casing on a stump over there. I'll bet people passing by this way will wonder how it got there, or where it came from."

"Don't Uncle Mech want it?"

"Dad, can we have the old tire?"

"Yea, but I don't want to take it with us. It'll be a nuisance."

Several times in later years, when I passed that way on expeditions of my own, I saw the old casing hanging there. I'd stop and let my horse rest—remembering.

Uncle Mech soon had the engine running again, ready to make a start if possible on the loose slickrock. All of us got behind to push. Somehow the wheels found traction, and the machine went bouncing and skidding up the grade, leaving the four of us stranded. We prayed it wouldn't blow another tire. Uncle Mech didn't stop until he topped out a half mile farther up the trail. We had to walk to where he waited for us.

From the top of Timber Hill we could see Stoney Pass, a bleak saddle between two higher peaks. Somehow Uncle Mech, with the help of the rest of us, was going to try and drive an automobile over it and on down the other side to Silverton, Colorado. There had never been an automobile on Silverton's streets. If we could do it, we'd be the first to put one there. So far the trip had been rough enough by any measure. But the pass high on the horizon looked impossible for anything other than teams or saddle stock.

Everybody was dry and warm by the time we'd conquered Timber Hill. Lost Trail Creek was miles behind and out of mind. The old wagon trail dipped down into the Rio Grand Canyon again for one final caper with the river. In the next mile the road crossed the stream thirteen times. It would have been no problem for teams and wagons, but for a car it was a disaster course. At this elevation, close to timber-line, the river is small but the bed is a jumble of boulders. Although Dad had had the road crew remove the largest of them, those fords were still no place for an automobile.

The car stalled in the first ford, but we finally worked it out onto the other bank. I knew there were at least twelve more fords, and I began to wonder if we'd get the car stuck in all of them. Splashing around in that ice cold water was no fun. In fact this expedition was losing a lot of its glamour for me, in fact the going had become a lot of cold, wet, hard work. Uncle Mech decided he'd better put the tire chains on for better traction. Even so, the car stalled in at least half the crossings.

Mr. McGuire said it for all of us. "Gentlemen," he said, "we'd just as well drive right up the center of the river. It'll save us the trouble of getting in and out of the damned thing all the time."

But we kept going, following the trail in and out of the river from one side to the other. Finally the car crawled out of the last ford like a tired old turtle. From there to Watson's Cabin the road was dry—what a relief. The county road crew was camped there, and the cook invited us in for a warm meal. He gave us roast beef, brown gravy, hot biscuits and coffee.

Watson's Cabin, named after the builder, is an old roadhouse built before the turn of the century. Although long abandoned, it's still used as a campsite. Logs from the caved-in buildings make hearty firewood. In those early days, it had been a refuge on the mountain for both man and beast. The only connection the San Juan country had with the outside world was over Stoney Pass to Creede, Colorado, sixty miles by wagon road that was little more than a trail. But the old timers had the guts and strength to overcome the hardships. Now a power driven machine was about to test its strength against the mountain barrier. The old roadhouse and those who used it had played their roles and gone their way. I wonder what the Squire would have said, had he stepped out his front door and found an automobile standing there. The oldsters who claimed to have known Squire Watson said he was a salty old boy.

Mr. McGuire was busy with his camera and notebook. Tug and I liked him. He always took time to tell us why he did things that way, and answer our questions. Sometimes it was hard to keep up with him, but we tried. Uncle Mech, as usual, checked the car over from end to end, making sure it was ready for the final effort—to top Old Stoney Pass in plain sight a scant two miles away but a long ways up. The road crew lined up to have their pictures taken and give us a cheery send-off.

"You think the car can do it, Tug?" I asked anxiously.

"Maybe not. Looks awful high and steep from down here. The road didn't look that steep and rough last month when we came over the pass on horseback."

We made a good start. The car clawed its way up around the first and second switchbacks, tires slipping and squealing on the slick rocks and the boiling radiator sending up a jet of steam. Timberline was almost a thousand feet below us now, and the motor was losing power fast because of the light air pressure. Mr. McGuire thought there must be some way to adjust the carburetor to compensate for the high elevation. Uncle Mech said it couldn't be done outside a shop equipped with the proper tools. So we struggled on.

Then a short way from the summit the engine gave up. It was running all right, but it just didn't have power to push the car any higher. There we were, almost on the crest of Old Stoney, and couldn't move an inch.

Uncle Mech looked at Dad. "Louie," he said, "We're going over that pass if I have to carry this machine over piece by piece. I won't drive back down that river. I've had enough of that. Besides, we're too close to a win to back up now."

"Well, let it set a few minutes and cool off, Mech, before you start taking it apart. The car smells like its too hot to handle anyhow."

Dad stepped up on a bank for a better look back down toward Watson's Cabin. He smiled and said "They'll be here in a few minutes Mech."

"They" were a team of big draft horses coming up the hill behind us. Dad had had the foresight to order the team to follow us clear to the top, just in case the automobile couldn't make it without help.

I'll never forget that team. Each horse weighed better than eighteen hundred pounds. Beautiful, proud dapple grays, so alike it was hard to tell them apart. Uncle Mech grinned at Dad. "You've still got your hand in, Louie. Right now that team is sure welcome." Mr. McGuire let out a whoop of joy when he saw them coming around a bend behind us. He snatched up his camera and started shooting pictures. Each horse had a singletree and chain hanging from his hams, the chain links tinkling a tune as they moved along. A feeling of guilt surged over me. Horses had always been my love, and I had forsaken them for this juggernaut of steel and rubber! I think in my kid way I began to realize a truth. Machines you admire and respect for their power and the tasks they're able to lift from men's shoulders. But a horse you loved.

It took some quiet coaxing to get the big fellows past the car. There wasn't much room. But they trusted old Gil their skinner and moved by, eyes rolling, ears twitching nervously, and their nostrils flaring. They didn't like the smell of gasoline and hot motor oil.

Tug was a bit let down at having to have a boost from a team to get the car over Stoney Pass. His dad's automobile was Tug's pride and to have it fail so close to the summit was hard to take. We learned later the carburetor could have been set easily for high altitudes, restoring much of the engine's power. That made Tug feel better; both of us knew the machine could have climbed over the pass if its crew had been wise enough to make an adjustment on the carburetor and give it a chance.

Me—I was proud of those horses that could pull more than a thirty horsepower motor. Horsepower, as applied to engines, was a puzzle to me. Tug didn't know how it worked either. But I knew the two horses Gil was hitching to the front of the car could and would pull it to the top of the pass. That was enough for me.

"Doctor, can you keep that machine on the road while the team's pulling it?" Gil asked skeptically. "It's got no wagon tongue to it."

"Sure, Gil, I can steer all right while the team pulls—no trouble."

"Will the brakes hold it from rolling backwards when the team stops to blow?"

"The brakes are good, Gil. They're okay. They'll hold it. There's no danger for the horses. Besides, Louie and McGuire will walk behind and block the wheels if we need to."

"All right. Can I sit on the front mud guard to drive?"

"Sure."

"We'll make it to the top easy enough, Doctor."

And we did. The horses had to stop and blow a few times. Dad, Mr. McGuire, Tug and I walked along ready to slam a big rock behind a rear wheel if it was needed. On some of the sharper pitches we pushed a bit too.

By 3:00 p.m., there we were with an automobile perched right on top of Stoney Pass like a tom cat on a telephone pole—12,500 feet above sea level. Near the top the grade had eased up some and we'd made fairly good time. The trick now was how to get it down the other side.

Gil unhitched the horses and led them aside. "There she is Doctor. It's all down hill from here. That contraption better have good hold-backs to it. The bottom's a hell of a long ways down there. Let me get the team back down the road a bit before you start that thing up—they ain't been weaned off hay and oats yet."

Gil shook hands all-round and mounted the off horse. We watched them start back to camp. Gil had a bill in his pocket that hadn't been there when he came up the mountain.

"Gee Tug, we'd better be ready to jump at any time going down this side. Are you scared?"

"Nope. Dad will stop and let the brakes cool of if they get hot—can't be any worse than what we been through." Tug was getting his cockiness back, now that the horses were gone.

"Yea, but what if he can't stop after we start down? That road goes down hill awful fast. I'm going to be ready to jump."

"Me too," Tug admitted.

After the usual picture taking we loaded up and Uncle Mech eased the car into the first down-hill pitch. He was an experienced driver, but I noticed he kept glancing down into the canyon depths. All of us sat stiffly on our seats, hardly knowing what to expect. Up to now we'd fought to move the car against steep grades, across rivers, and through hub-deep mud. This sudden reversal of forces was frightening. If given a chance, the mountain could hurl the car forward, like a projectile, destroying it and its passengers as well.

Stoney Creek Gulch lives up to its name in every respect. From the summit down to where it joins Cunningham Canyon it's a steep and rugged defile, dropping 2,500 feet in less than four miles. On the west side of the Continental Divide the wagon trail had been improved slightly because of mining activity. It was never, however, intended for automobiles. We worked our way down slowly, stopping now and then to roll boulders out of the way and cool the brakes. Once they had to be tightened. But by four o'clock Uncle Mech was jockeying the car around the last hairpin curves of Stoney Gulch, and the car rolled out onto the county road in Cunningham Canyon.

Uncle Mech adjusted his hat, cocking it over one ear a bit more. Dad had a big smile on his face, and Mr. McGuire relaxed on his seat beside Tug and me. We were all too exhausted to say much, but we knew we'd won. Silverton was only a short distance down the valley with a good road to drive on.

Not only was this Croxton-Keeton, 4 cylinder, 30 h.p. car the first auto into Silverton, it was the first vehicle over what was to eventually become the Million Dollar Highway. Today that highway is Highway 550 and crosses Red Mountain between Silverton and Ouray through some of the most spectacular scenery in the country. The picture is taken at Bear Creek Falls near Ouray, in the year 1910. Daymar Quarnstrom Collection, San Juan County Historical Society.

Silverton awaited us. Word had been telephoned in from a mine that the car was down off the mountain and headed for town. It seemed to me that everybody in town had turned out to celebrate the ushering in of a new era and to welcome the first automobile to the San Juan and Silverton.

Dynamite exploded on a hillside above town. The band was assembled in front of city hall, doing their best to be heard above the wild cheering as Uncle Mech braked to a stop with a flourish and a long blast on the horn. There were people in that crowd who had never seen an automobile except in published pictures. It was better than a Labor Day celebration.

But let Mr. McGuire tell it..."As we entered the city bombs were fired from a prominent hilltop, and with the clanging of bells and music from the band, we drew up in front of city hall surrounded by a concourse of excited and enthusiastic citizens. Here, a royal welcome awaited us. In fact, so demonstrative were the citizens in showing their appreciation, and so genuine and hearty was the reception accorded us, that for the first time during our whole trip we began to wake up and realize that possibly we might have accomplished something worthwhile after all. In front of city hall some of the writer's old hunting friends appeared—among them, Brice and Harry Patterson of Pagosa Springs, and Ray Cooper of Silverton, while others to crowd their way to the car and greet us were W.N. Searcy, Mr. Jury, Mayor Allen, Otto Mears, 'The Pathfinder of the Rockies', Mr. Joyce and others."

For years afterward the San Juan country remained hostile to automobiles. Old Stoney Pass has never been subdued by a highway. The rocky old trail we sweated over is still there, much the same. Not until seven years later in 1918 was a road, with grades easy enough for cars, built over a more feasible route into Silverton. Dad helped to build it, realizing at long last his dream was finally coming true. Three resolute men and two venturesome kids brought the first automobile to the San Juan over roads that were scarcely more than a trail, and against odds that seemed insurmountable.

Two days after our arrival in Silverton I helped Tug stow his gear in the car as he made ready to start the trip home. Not back over Stoney and the Continental Divide but by roads kinder to automobiles. When he'd finished packing everything the rifle was still standing against the fence. Tug picked the gun up and looked it over carefully. Then he handed it to me with the scabbard, ammunition, and gun oil.

"Here Lew, would you like to keep it? Dad promised me a new repeater when we get home. Ask your father if he'll let you have it."

All Dad said was, "You've been shooting that gun all summer. If you can't handle a gun by now, you never will."

Yes, it had been a good summer, filled with many firsts for all of us. Dad had brought the first automobile to Silverton—the hard way. Daydreams of his erupting into reality. And I had a first too, tucked under my arm. And to paraphrase an old ballad—"I Had Memories Pleasant On My Mind."

A photograph, not of the first car, but of the first aeroplane to land in Silverton. The time is May, 1935, and the place is the corner of 8th and Greene. Raymond Doud Photo, Jim Bell/Gerald Glanville Collection.

Entertainment, like gold, was where you found it. The kids are out in front of the Gem Theatre and the Silverton Standard newspaper, taken around 1912. Arline Clifford Hembree Collection, San Juan County Historical Society.

Kentuck's Last Ride

He was Kentucky Blue Ridge, transplanted in the high Rockies of the Southwest. I am sure no other nickname but "Kentuck" would have suited him so well. Tall and gaunt and about fifty, he reminded me of a suit on a wire coat hanger that had somehow sprouted feet. Strangers were inclined to smile a little when they first met him. Sometimes, if the smiles were patronizing, his blue eyes could turn hard as crystals. But mostly, they sparkled with fun, and every kid in town was his friend.

Kentuck had the whole town buzzing the summer he learned to drive his first car, a brand new Studebaker Big Six, green as a grasshopper and fitted with a California top. It was about as fine a car as ever rolled up and down Silverton's dusty streets. Kentuck did himself and the little mining town of Silverton proud when he bought it. The fact that his bank account, like all the rest of ours, was never very stable had the back-fence teletype going full blast. Whether he was in the chips or not depended on his luck at leasing and contracting. But the neighborhood kids had a bonanza. They flocked to the car like homing pigeons, sure of a welcome and a big helping of fun to top it off. Kentuck's transition from horses and wagons to gasoline and engines didn't work out too well, and it gave the town's citizenry some concern. He didn't drive fast, and it bothered him that he couldn't see the front bumper. Usually, when he remembered it was there, it was too late. He never overcame the habit of driving directly to where he wanted to go, much as he'd drive a team of mules. It was confusing to other drivers—but there weren't that many in town then.

The trouble was that tire tracks appeared on the Courthouse lawn, and now and then a fireplug became a fountain, much to the delight of the kids. More likely than not, there would have been a half-dozen or so in the car at the time of the action.

It was a bit unnerving for the minister and the congregation when the lights went out while the deacon was taking up the collection at Sunday evening services. And at times, the ladies complained of the telephone service, especially if they had a good thing going over the wire. All of it was the result of utility poles and equipment that failed to withstand the impact of Kentuck's big Studebaker.

Walking down the street early one morning, I saw his automotive misadventures come to an abrupt end. The event was a fitting demise to his errant driving career. There was nothing I, nor anyone else, could have done to prevent it.

He came out of his house, apparently intending to drive to town, so I thought I'd hit him up for a ride. After a few tries, he got the engine going and slowly—in low gear—drove out of his driveway to the street. But he never made the turn. Instead, he went straight across, pulling back on the steering wheel and yelling, "Whoa!", as if he was riding a runaway stage. He was evidently too confused to do anything but hold on.

Judge Wesson's back yard was directly opposite Kentuck's driveway. The car seemed almost too deliberate as it climbed over the curb and sidewalk. The judge's high board fence bent in a graceful arc before it went down with a splintering crash. Still the juggernaut was not satisfied. It chewed up the fence boards as it moved on, with Kentuck petrified at the wheel.

The Wesson coal shed was next. It offered little more resistance than the fence. The front end of the Studebaker disappeared inside the collapsing shed with Kentuck still at the wheel. Finally, he began to take part in the action. His voice came out of the dust and shambles in a fine combination of hog-calling, prayer-shouting, and just plain mule-skinner cussing.

Inside, the automobile rammed into a good sized pile of coal. It wasn't high enough to stop it entirely, and the front wheels went up and over the mound. At the same time, the radiator and the car top pushed the shed roof up off the walls. Then the roof broke in two, and the whole shed fell apart. But the coal pile was too much, and the engine stalled, leaving the front end of the car up on top like a pussy on a cushion. One headlight was gone entirely; the other was bent and staring down the far side of the mound. Mrs. Wesson's wash tubs were crumpled under the front axle, and a garden hose festooned the radiator.

Still, there was no lull in the action. Wesson himself took charge of the proceedings and was doing his level best to get at Kentuck with the kitchen stove poker. But the wreckage hindered his foot work considerably, and Kentuck's dodging ability kept a substantial amount of Studebaker between himself and the judge.

All the ruckus brought out the neighbors in force. Some of them thought things had gone far enough and disarmed the judge. It reduced the conflict to mere name-calling and arm waving.

Kentuck did his best to explain how it happened, while everyone inspected the damage to the automobile and to Wesson's property.

It was an enjoyable outing for everyone, 'though a bit early in the morning. There were plenty of willing hands in the crowd, so at the judge's request, they gathered round and rolled the car down off the coal pile and out to the curb. The Studebaker looked like an old soldier back from a hard campaign.

Kentuck was a good craftsman when the occasion demanded, and there was no question about the fact that he had an obligation to the judge. It was no surprise to anyone in town that, in due time, he had the fence and the shed repaired. And he had some help, too. The older youngsters pitched in with their usual enthusiasm, especially when a project concerned the Studebaker. According to the judge, the automobile was in hock until the repairs were finished.

Kentuck never drove a car again, and things became downright dull about town. But not for the kids; they could always find someone to drive for them.

Of course they needed a little help with the gas now and then.

Shenanigans

It was apparent I wouldn't get a ride to town with Kentuck that morning. His involvement with the judge was likely to occupy his attention for some time. So I walked on down the street.

Nowhere else have I found anything so beautiful as a bright August morning in the high country. Sunshine comes down from over the peaks in a golden flood, and the air turns warm and gentle on your face. There's a muffled rhythm of life, more felt than heard, that mutes the strident notes of man's endeavors. Just to have been in a world that was clean was enough.

I was about to turn down main street when I noticed Bill Dennis (just Bill to everyone in town), and a stranger I'd never seen before, working on Bill's tank truck. They had the rig parked in his backyard, and were pouring water into it with a ten-gallon measuring bucket.

Bill was an enterprising gent with a reputation for pulling shenanigans. He was also our first and only oil dealer, and operated a small bulk plant at the south end of town. He used a ton and a half flat-bed truck with a removable tank for his deliveries. Tankers as we know them today were unheard of.

It looked as though there might be a buck or two in it for me, if I could get into the action. I got in all right.

The first thing I knew, I was packing the ten gallons of water up the ladder and dumping it into the tank. Bill and the gentleman—who turned out to be an inspector—kept the tally, and sat out a long rest. Eventually, we filled it, and the gent made his calculations. He gave Bill a clearance on the tank's capacity, bundled up his equipment and was on his way. I was glad to see him go. Filling the truck's tank with a ten gallon bucket wasn't my idea of a good job.

"Well," Bill said, "I got a gasoline truck full of water. Tell you what we'd better do. I'll drive over on main street, and we can open the drain valves and let it run down the gutter."

Silverton is one of those mountain towns blessed with an abundant water supply. Only the main street had cement gutters. The city allowed a small stream of water to flow from an open fireplug to keep them washed clean. So Bill thought he'd just drain the truck tank there, too.

We drove up the alley and turned into the main street in front of the Town Hall and stopped with the truck's back end over the gutter. I got out to open the drain valves.

"Open 'em wide," Bill shouted. "We don't have all day. I have to deliver gas this morning."

A three-and-a-half inch free-flow valve discharges a reasonable stream and the tank had one on each side where the discharge hoses connected. I spun 'em wide open and stepped back to watch the results. It was anything but what I'd expected.

Bill put the truck in gear and drove right down the middle of the main street, with water spewing out in two big streams—one on each side of the truck.

If he intended it for a joke, he got his money's worth. Things started to happen immediately.

The town clerk heard me yelling for Bill to stop. He took one look at the truck rolling down the street with two great streams of what he thought was gasoline pouring out of the tank valves. He panicked and turned in a fire alarm.

Volunteer fire department communications are not too good at times. Men popped out of most every door. Some, who didn't realize what was happening, ran for the fire truck at the Town Hall. Others took in the situation at a glance and ducked back inside, locking their doors and pulling blinds. People on the sidewalk were shouting and pointing to the truck trying to make Bill understand he was spilling gasoline all over the street. But he just smiled and waved back, driving along and clearing the street as he went.

In the meantime, enough firemen had arrived to man the community's fire truck. They dashed out to the middle of the street before they realized no one knew where the fire was. When word finally came through about Bill's runaway gas truck, they went after him, down the supposedly gas-soaked street. I've often wondered since just what they expected to do, driving down a street that was a potential holocaust. But after Bill they went, their old vehicle throwing mud like a manure spreader.

Clinky, the restaurant's owner and day cook, came out to see what all the rumpus was about. One look was enough for her.

"My God!" she said. "He's going to cremate the whole town!"

A large husky woman, she never had any trouble making herself understood. She held the restaurant door open and shouted for a few women and kids who were slow in getting off the street to get inside before the whole damn place went to hell in a puff of smoke.

By this time, Bill and the fire truck had the street pretty much to themselves. Not a soul remained in sight except in front of the grocery store where a string of pack mules was loading supplies for a mine in the high back country. Ordinarily, a pack mule is fairly quiet and docile. But they don't like shouting people, fire sirens or gasoline trucks that speed by with water spewing all over everything. Once he's aroused and scared, a mule is a four-footed devil. Fifteen of them tied end to end by their lead ropes—and spooked—are a packer's despair.

By the time the fire truck arrived at that point, the whole street was blocked with bucking and braying mules. So far, the firemen had no fire to fight, so they joined the packers in an attempt to get the situation under control. However, they were somewhat handicapped.

Taming a mule is a two-fisted job. A man trying to keep a big red fireman's hat on his head with one hand while he holds a loco mule with the other is a little too involved for good results. The casualties were running pretty high for both hats and firemen.

My luck was none too good either. At the end of a lead rope I'd somehow got hold of was a big brown Roman-nosed mule. I saw the name "Maude" printed in white letters on the front pack-saddle tree. Asking the lady for a dance was not on my mind at all. But she led off, and we pirouetted gracefully around the fire truck a time or two. She had a big weight advantage, and I'd say her enthusiasm was tops. Although she had four feet to my two, she tried to be fair and put only one or two on the ground at a time. But she was erratic as hell with the others. Then for variety, she wound up smashing her load against the truck.

Under normal circumstances, Maude was a very good pack animal. She usually carried the eggs and perishables. That was a mistake this day. I finally got her tied up and left, walking away from a dripping mess of eggs without so much as a good-bye.

Word got around that what everyone thought was gasoline was just water. As if by magic, the street filled as quickly as it had emptied. There were a few angry faces, but mostly everyone enjoyed the excitement, since there was no real danger. The firemen came in for some good-natured ribbing. Maude and her pals had broken a few lead ropes and a case of eggs had to be replaced. But that was about the extent of the damage.

I walked on down to the bulk plant. I had a thing or two to tell Bill, and I anticipated the telling with relish. On the doorlatch, he'd tied a brown envelope with my name on it. Inside were two silver dollars and a note.

"I'll be out of town for a day or so," it said.

Well, Bill knew the town would cool off quickly. He'd had a good laugh and no doubt would get a little drunk-wherever he was. When he came home, all would be forgotten, and we'd sit back and wonder what the next shenanigan would be.

I had two silver dollars in my pocket, and it was time to see if Clinky had any chili for lunch.

The Salvation Army entertains on the main street of Silverton in the early 1920's. Raymond Doud Photo, Jim Bell/Gerald Glanville Collection.

Clinky

A little after noon, I pulled the bulk plant shack's door shut, made sure it was locked, and drove up town in Bill's old pickup. The morning had been all I could ask for by way of activity, and I was getting hungry.

Clinky's restaurant was always a good stop. The food was plain but good. Often the impromptu floor show she'd put on left nothing to be desired by way of entertainment. One thing a person could be sure of—Clinky was always the star.

I plunked myself down on a bar-stool and looked up to find Clinky staring at me. Her eyes were cold as blue ice, and I got a chill, even if it was August.

"What the hell did you have to do with that fracas this morning?" she asked.

"Oh, that darn pack mule I tried to quiet down smashed a case of eggs on the fire truck," I replied. "That was a mess. They were all over her and the truck, too. Why? What about it?"

"You wasn't with that Irish clown on the gas truck?"

"No. Like I told you, Maude and I fixed up a whole case of eggs. Now will you get me a bowl of chili?"

"Sure, if you got money to pay for it."

"I got money."

"Where's Bill now?"

"I don't know. He left a note saying he'd gone out of town on business. Didn't say where."

"You can bet your worthless hide he'd better be out of town," she said. "The man that kills that Irish clown ought to be made a Saint." Then she stamped back to the kitchen for my chili.

I was getting along just fine with my lunch. Clinky stood behind the bar with her back turned to me, glaring out the front windows. She had her hands on her hips and the ever-ready bar towel draped over her shoulder. From the shaggy yellow hair on her head to the tennis shoes she wore for comfort, she was one solid gal. A little wide and a little short, but Clinky never took second money from anyone. She hadn't said anything for a few minutes. I looked around to see what could keep her quiet for so long.

Early that spring, some one had found a tiny bear cub. The little devil had become the pride and joy of the men at the mine. He was as fat and spoiled a little runt as one could imagine. Chico, a mine cook, seemed to be the cub's godfather and brought him into town often. Tourists and the kids were delighted with his antics. He knew where the drug store and the restaurant were. He'd cry and beg and pull on his chain until he'd been fed all the ice cream and pie he could hold. If some one gave him a cone, he'd stand on his hind feet like a little man, hold the cone with his front paws, and literally dance with ecstasy while he ate it. Clinky took a dim view of bear cubs, mine cooks, and tourists. The money tourists spent in the restaurant was fine, but it didn't raise her opinion of them one bit. The less she saw of bear cubs and mine cooks, the better.

Outside, Chico was feeding the cub a box of fresh, red strawberries, one at a time. A crowd had gathered round to watch the fun.

"That damn hash wrecker better not bring that stinking cub in here," Clinky said. "If he does, I'll wash both of 'em down the sewer."

When Clinky set her jaw after a declaration of any kind, it always reminded me of a wedge plow with the point squared off.

"I don't think he will, Clinky. I heard he said your cooking gave the cub a belly ache."

The end of her bar towel cracked viciously just short of my ear.

"Now wait a minute," I said. "I only told you what I heard. Some day, you're going to swat the wrong man with that rag and get your butt paddled good."

"After spoon-feeding the likes of you, it'll be a pleasure," she retorted.

I thought it best not to push the subject; Clinky wasn't in a good mood. Outside, the tourists were enjoying the cub and taking pictures. One very large lady—dressed in tight knee pants and a shirt—wanted to have her picture taken while she held the chain and fed him. Chico tried to explain to her that it took some experience to handle the bear while he was being fed. But if she wished, he'd hold the chain, and she could feed him.

No, that wouldn't do at all. She must have her picture taken while she held a real live bear and fed it. At last, Chico gave in and handed her the chain and the berries.

"Hold him as far away from yourself as you can," he advised her.

Her friends got their cameras going, and it looked as though things were working out all right. Then it happened.

She tried to get the cub to stand on his hind legs and beg for a strawberry. But bears don't do that unless they're in a cage or held back by a chain. The little devil could smell the berries somewhere above him and grabbed the lady's leg and started to climb.

A bear cub is the last word in agility, and the lady's ample leg was easy to climb. He made it clear to her waist before anyone could stop him, his claws drawing a little blood now and then as he went. Chico and some of the bystanders took him away as quickly as they could, but it was a bit late.

The poor woman was hurt and frightened. After some good loud screaming, she decided to pass out. She did it beautifully, and three or four citizens lowered her gently to the sidewalk.

Clinky—ever a woman of action—went out with a pitcher of ice-water to revive her. I shuddered when the water hit the poor soul full in the face. I've seen good, hard dog fights broken up with a single bucket of that liquid ice. I suppose one could question which was more painful to the lady—the water or the cub. But there was no way she could ignore the ice water, and she was up and about immediately.

Having put things to rights outside, Clinky turned to come back into the restaurant just as Chico and the cub slipped through the door. She come bouncing in after them, waving her water pitcher like a shillelagh.

"Chico!" she yelled. "Get that damned animal out of my restaurant before I kill the both of you! Go hide in the shack across the alley. I'll send somebody to let you know when the coast is clear. Those fools outside will be looking for you in a minute. I don't want your stinking mess around here if they find you."

She was right. A group of angry tourists and a native or two came in demanding the bear and its master. A woman had been badly mauled by the beast, said a spokesman, and it was high time such a dangerous animal was done away with. The handler and the bear had been seen entering the restaurant, and it was the duty of the proprietor to turn the beast and its master over to them.

Clinky faced the committee from just inside the door. "Now, listen," she said. "This is a place where people eat and not a stinking zoo. It's not a hangout for 'Joblows' who think they can push the locals around because they have a plugged nickel to spend. If you people want something to eat, sit down, and I'll serve you. If you're bear hunting, get the hell out into the woods. That's where they are!"

Clinky's formidable when she gets excited and takes a stand on a question. I've never known her to lose an argument or a fight. She was too much for the vigilantes; they hastily withdrew to the sidewalk outside. She looked them over silently from the doorway, but her contempt was loud and clear.

I sat down again to finish my coffee. A few minutes later she shoved a heaping plate of cold griddle-cakes and syrup in front of me.

"I don't want that junk," I told her.

"It's not for you, you stupid oaf. Pay for your chili and then take the stack of cakes out back and feed the cub. They'll kill the poor little devil feeding him nothing but ice cream and fat women. And give that misguided biscuit mechanic a cup of coffee if he wants it."

Clinky's that way—rough as a piece of granite—but she's not too bad. If she wants to kill you, she'll give you an aspirin to ease the pain, and then pay for your funeral.

"And while you're at it," she called after me, "Get that old pickup truck of Bill's and take the cub and that bum back to the mine. Those cushion-pushers might try it again. If they do, and go to the mine for their bear hunting, Man! That would be a party worth going to!"

Problem Solved

About four o'clock, I parked Bill's pickup in front of the hardware store and went in to see what brother Bob had on his mind.

"Where you been?" he said. "I've had kids looking all over town for you."

"Ah, I took Chico and his cub bear back to the mine. They got into a ruckus up at Clinky's joint and had to get out of town for a while."

"Well, if you're through with your good turns for the day, mind the store while I get some work done on the books."

It's nice to work in a hardware store. There are guns, fishing tackle and all the things a man needs. When the stuff is all about you on the shelves, and in the showcases under your care, it's like you owned it. You get the same feeling when a two-bit slot machine dumps the jackpot in your hand.

I was standing up front at the gun case, fondling a new Winchester lever-action 30-40. To own it was a long-cherished dream. It takes something unusual to divert a man's attention from a fine rifle, or firearm of any kind, for that matter. But across the street, a crowd was gathering in front of the Circle Route Garage. I carefully locked the rifle away, dropped the gun case key in the cash register and took off. I had to get closer to the action.

Just before the door closed behind me, Bob yelled, "Where the hell you going?" But you don't pay much attention to brothers, especially one who is very well able to take care of himself, and does.

The object of everyone's interest was a brand new Model T Ford coupe, as shiny and black as a ferret's eye. The only break in its sable splendor: four nickel-plated wheel bearing caps. They kind of reminded me of silver buttons on a black sateen shirt. A new car in town was always an event, and everybody who wasn't too busy gathered 'round to inspect and comment. Glass-enclosed cars were the newest thing. There were only a few in the county, so the crowd had a genuine interest in the new coupe.

Fatso, one of our most eligible bachelors, claimed to be the proud owner. Sitting demurely beside him was his big interest of the moment. The lady seemed quite embarrassed by all the attention from the local gentry. I'm sure she wished Fat would drive on, but it's practically impossible to set a car in motion with people standing close around it.

I noticed Sully and Pete, two active young promoters of civic affairs, were moving rapidly from man to man through the crowd. To each one they explained something very carefully and received a smile and nod in return.

In a short time about twenty of the stalwarts had gathered in a tight group around the Ford. At a given signal from Sully, they took hold of the car's bumpers, running boards and fenders, and lifted it straight up in the air. They held it high enough so Sully and Pete could place a fifty-gallon oil barrel, on end, under each wheel. Gently, they settled the car on its perch—then faded away. It was astonishing to see how smoothly the two imps had engineered the whole thing.

It delighted the crowd, and they waited around to see how Fat would get himself and his lady back on the ground. As for the car, that was another problem.

Fat took the prank with good humor. Opening the door, he jumped out and went around to lift his lady friend down. She arranged her dress to prevent any undue exposure, and Fat set her carefully on the ground. I thought it took him quite a long time to do the job, but then, she was a pretty gal. Somehow, a lot of shapely leg showed up, and the boys voiced their approval heartily. Fat walked his lady home, then came back to face the second part of his problem: How to get the coupe off the barrels.

Figuring that Sully and Pete would get the same bunch together and set the car down, I went home to supper and a clean shirt. There were a few chores to tend to about the house, and I didn't get back down town until after eight o'clock.

At night, the action of a mining town moves indoors to the bright lights, gambling tables and bars. The streets are deserted and fairly quiet, except when a door swings open and the noise comes blasting out into the night. Or some rounder staggers to another saloon to try his luck or buy a drink.

I dropped in at the Hub Saloon to pick up the latest dope from Hal, the barkeep. He told me Fat's car was still up on the barrels. Hal said Fat had been trying all evening to get the car down but with no luck. He'd been buying drinks for the bums and doing everything he could to get enough of them together at one time to lift the car back down. None of them actually refused help, Hal said. It was just that Fat couldn't find them all at once. I thought I'd look him up and maybe give a hand.

In a joint we called The Laundry (if you had anything when you went in, they cleaned you before you came out), I found old Fat sitting in a chair. He'd had a few too many and was all but passed out. It seemed to me the guys had gone too far. A practical joke is fun, but this one had wound down to a mess and wasn't funny any more. I thought it time to square the thing away.

I managed to get the Ford's keys from Fat, then left him there to sleep it off. I needed a telephone, so I headed for Clinky's restaurant and hopped up on a counter stool close to the phone booth. Jimmy, Clinky's old man, runs the night shift. Without a word, he set a cup of coffee in front of me and went back into the kitchen. Now if I could just get a minute or two when the place was empty.

A cup of coffee later, my chance came. The place had cleared out, and I dived into the phone booth. It don't take long to turn in a fire alarm. I told the operator, "The Circle Route Garage is on fire! Ring the bell!"

"My God!" she gasped.

I was back on my stool drinking coffee before the fire alarm sounded at Town Hall. Jimmy came to the kitchen's swinging doors and gravely announced, "There's a fire someplace."

That was a very lengthy speech for Jimmy. Clinky did the talking for the two of them, so Jimmy didn't have to bother with it. But he was hep to everything that happened on the street. I think he saw me in the phone booth and knew something was afoot. Anyway, it was time to go. I dropped a dime on the counter and took off.

A little while before the street had been quiet, except for the foot traffic from saloon to saloon. A mob seemed to have sprung up out of the dust. I worked my way in close to Fat's Ford, and yelled as loud as I could: "Get this car the hell out of here!"

It worked like magic. A bunch took hold and the car just floated off the barrels and across the street to safety before they even set the wheels on the ground. Having saved Fat's valuable property from complete destruction, the noble firemen swarmed back to fight the garage fire. Trouble was, nobody could find it. But it gave me a chance to sneak away with the Ford and go get Fat.

The barkeep at The Laundry helped me. We piled Fat into his coupe, and I drove him home to his room by the back streets. He gave me all the help he could, and I got him to bed.

It had taken a little time to get Fat settled for the night. Back on the main street, the crowd was thinning out. Firemen were cleaning up and putting their equipment away for the second time that day. I heard some pretty pointed remarks about clowns who turned in false alarms. It was better for me not to stick around; somebody might start asking questions. I wasn't a fireman anyway.

I drifted over to the Hub to hear the latest slant on things from Hal. He said the night cop and the fire chief had been in and left word. The next false alarm that was turned in, they'd run the guy down if it took all night, and see to it that he got thirty days without bail.

There was a wide grin on Hal's face. He liked old Fatso, too.

Johnny-Mac

Johnny-Mac was 230 pounds of trained athlete. He taught junior high math and manual training and coached the school's athletics. He made basketball teams that were champions. He made trackmen who were winners, and he made young men out of some pretty raw material. The stars on the banner that hangs in the old high school auditorium (I hope it's still there) tell the story loud and clear. With Johnny-Mac the action was fast and good all the way.

As a junior high and first-year senior high student, I couldn't compete with the upperclassmen in athletics (they were the stars and heroes of the old school), but down in the shop, with hammer and saw, I held my own with the best of them. The skills Johnny-Mac taught me have been a lifelong treasure.

He was a boy's man. In a rough-and-tumble he could handle any four of us, and often did. We'd find ourselves pinned to the mat with Johnny-Mac sitting on top of the pile laughing at us.

When he'd catch us in some devilment, we paid up on the spot, and the incident was forgotten. No trivial hangovers, no retribution or silly penitence with Johnny-Mac, you paid your bill as you went and that was that. But if we were in the right and wrongly accused, no bunch of youngsters ever had a better friend. He stood by us and we trusted him. He was not in the habit of losing an argument, a contest, or a game. With him we won.

In this world it seems we must have some unpleasantness to balance the good. We had it. A professor of science on the senior high faculty became a major problem for our upperclassmen, and for some of us lesser fry as well. The gentlemen was a real intellectual and a complete egotist in the bargain. At times his comments and observations were so vitriolic and condescending he was beyond endurance. But a teacher was a teacher and could do no wrong.

It all came to a head one fine spring day. The upperclassmen who had taken all they could from him were in open rebellion. They decided to waylay the professor at noon, work him over thoroughly, and just maybe he'd get the message. Everyone knew they'd be expelled from school. Even Johnny-Mac would have to turn his back on them. But it was like someone said, "It's the army for us in a few weeks, so why not get in a little practice before we take on the 'Kaiser'?"

A small yellow and white cottage with a picket fence stood on a south corner of the schoolhouse block. The professor passed that way each day at lunch time, so the would-be thugs waited for him there. Each boy yanked a picket from the fence and held it behind him, out of sight.

Right on time, the professor came through the short-cut he always used, and turned down Reese Street. But he wasn't alone. Johnny-Mac was with him. He'd heard of the planned donnybrook and decided to take a hand in it. There was never a hint that they saw anything unusual in the line-up by the fence as they came down the street.

They came right down the line-up of half-scared tough guys, the professor nodding a greeting and Johnny-Mac plucking a picket from the hand of each lad as they went by. The professor never changed his pace—just walked casually on home to his lunch. He was a cool one, and it changed our attitude toward him to a grudging admiration.

Johnny-Mac laid his arm-load of pickets inside the gate and turned to face a bunch of overgrown kids who'd just missed doing a stupid thing. The hard glint in his eyes didn't match the casual tone of voice when he spoke.

"Listen fellows," he said, "The old lady's fence is in bad shape. She needs it to keep the stock off her flower beds. After class this afternoon, check out what tools you need from the manual training shop, and we'll set it up in good condition for her."

Although no word was spoken concerning a donnybrook that had faded away somehow, we knew well enough when we were home free. Johnny-Mac's message was plain and strong. "You'd better make sure you're a man before you take on a man's job."

By the end of the school year some of the upperclassmen were in uniform already. Johnny-Mac was gone, too, and the professor had gone East to a new school.

From time to time when I passed the little yellow cottage, I'd stop and test the fence to see if the pickets were still tight—they were. Johnny-Mac and his young men had done the job up right. Years afterward when I would pull a boo-boo at work and mess up a piece, it seemed I could hear him laugh and say, "You think you can save it?"

This is Silverton's old frame schoolhouse, pictured here at recess time in 1910. San Juan County Historical Society.

Pay Dirt

Early one clear, crisp Sunday morning in April, Pete Johnson and his side-kick Erik Giles were struggling to adjust after a wild night out on the town. They made a strange pair. Pete was always well groomed, small and precise, with his textbook English, and the perfect gentleman whether drunk or sober. Erik was everything Pete was not: big, rugged, and tough. Pete, however, was headman in their partnership and usually called the shots. Erik followed along to supply the brawn, when needed, and enjoy the fun. Both men were good-natured, born rounders.

The night-life of a booming high country mining camp like Silverton, Colorado, provided all the entertainment they could handle.

On the west side of town, church bells reminded the faithful that morning services were about to take up. Families dressed in Sunday finery made their way along rough board sidewalks. The ladies were stepping carefully, lest they catch a heel in a knothole or crack between the planks.

Some of their gentlemen escorts, a bit bleary-eyed but proper as sanctimonious church deacons passing the morning collection plate, paced along in step with their womenfolk.

Half of the old mining camp was waking up to a bright spring morning. The other half, the east side of town, including Main Street, was going to sleep. It had endured one of those wild nights, when payday happened to fall on a Saturday.

From sundown Saturday to sunup Sunday morning, gamblers, dance hall girls, and bartenders did their best to separate the payroll cash, completely and pleasantly, from the gents who'd earned it. The Mayor's Bank as some wit had dubbed the city jail, where a busy night-cop could deposit an overly enthusiastic reveler, did a good business.

By the time old Sol swept away the morning mist and flooded the little town with sunshine, a whiskey bottle had lost much of its magic. Most of Silverton's freewheeling spirits had sacked out.

Pete and Erik had been run out of the last dance hall they'd patronized. That is, Erik had. He was always more than willing to argue a point in contention. Pete had gone peaceably enough. If he happened to get mixed up in the rough stuff, it would be purely accidental. He depended on Erik's muscle to handle that part of the evening entertainment.

By some strange quirk of luck they hadn't been deposited in the Mayor's Bank, to satisfy a delinquent account that some night-cop figured they owed. Either there had been too much water in the bar-whiskey, or they'd spent too lavishly early in the evening. Pete and Erik were still on their feet while the action up and down the street had sizzled out like a wet fuse. Somehow the festivities had been disappointing.

They wandered disconsolately down a side lane toward the Animas River, more because it was easier to stroll down a gentle slope, than for any other reason. Near the end of the lane they found a small church the black folks in town had built beside the river.

It was the only church on that side of town. The front doors were thrown wide open invitingly, and a small congregation was singing the first hymn for the Sunday morning service.

Pete stopped and put his hand on Erik's arm.

"Listen, Erik, they're singing off key and I don't hear an instrument of any kind leading them. Do you? Come let us look in."

" Oh no, Pete. You and me has no business in there. The place'd fold up."

"Erik, I see a small organ there by the pulpit. We will go in. I will play, and you can pump for me. The congregation needs the organ music to lead them."

"Noth'n do'n, Pete. You pounded on the piano in half the joints in town last night. Ain't that enough?"

Erik, this is Sunday morning, we should be in church."

"Oh, I don't know Pete. I think this round you won't get to spit. And besides, I ain't a church goer."

"I'm going to play for their church service, Erik. Will you please pump the organ for me? Come, let us go in now. Do you have fifty cents for the collection plate?"

"Hell no! They threw us out of The Diamond Bell because we couldn't pay for that last round of drinks. You ain't so drunk you don't remember that?"

As Pete and Erik moved up the side aisle toward the altar, the singing slowly faded away. The minister and his congregation hardly know what to expect of their visitors. But a benevolent smile on Pete's good-natured face, and his polite manner was reassuring enough. There was nothing alarming about Erik either. He just shuffled along behind the little guy, looking like a sheep dog that had been caught asleep.

By way of an introduction, Pete said, "Reverend, I am Mr. Johnson and the gentleman with me is my friend, Mr. Giles. Sir, if you have no organist today, I will be happy to play the organ for you. And I'm sure Mr. Giles will pump for me."

Pete's offer was received gratefully, and the preacher bid them welcome. But he neglected to mention the hymns he'd selected for that Sunday's service. So Pete made his own selections.

He lead the congregation through the militant spiritual, "When The Saints Go Marching In." The second time around he had them singing in full voice. The third time they were clapping, and the excitement was building fast. Under any circumstance, Pete's performance on a piano or organ could bring down the house.

Inspired by the congregation's response, Pete rolled into "The Hallelujah Chorus" with a good swinging down beat. It brought his audience to its feet in a wild stamping, hand clapping ecstasy of religious fervor.

Erik had warmed up to his work at the organ pump handle too, giving Pete more air than he could use at the treadles and keyboard. Now and then when he peeked over the top of the organ to see how their team work was going, his grin was anything but cherubic. Pete and he had turned the Sunday worship service into a noisy shouting jamboree.

Outside, the neighborhood people gathered around expecting to see a riot spill out into the churchyard. Erik glanced up from his labor at the organ pump and saw a city cop standing in the front door. He hissed at Pete and pointed to the officer. All at once Pete's music lost its throbbing beat and slowed to a stately cadence. In a moment, excitement and noise slithered away like a punctured balloon.

The crowd pressed in closer to see what was going on, then funneled through the door, filling the church. Pete's music drew them in and held them. Realizing he was playing to a full house, he did it justice.

Later that morning while he and Erik sat drinking black coffee, sick and broke, Erik said, "Pete, I kind'a like a music-box it takes both of us to work. If I don't pump, you don't get a squeak out of that machine."

"I know, Erik. But right now a major chord in any key would split my head wide open. Let us go back on the hill as soon as we can. Agreed?"

"Sure, Pete. I been think'n, if that preacher can stand us, I'd like to put in a few rounds. This one didn't misfire on us. And that day cop had to back off when we spit the fuse. That never happened to us before."

"Very well, Erik. Next Sunday if we're in town, we will go to church. Do you think we can ignore The Diamond Bell, The Tremont, or The Bon Ton until we get there?"

"Sure, we never struck pay dirt, yet, in any of them joints."

This is a view of town in early 1900 showing the frame Catholic Church (circled) before it was moved close to the river and became a church for the Afro-Americans. The wooden structure was replaced with a brick one in the same spot and remains the Catholic Church today. Ray Doud photo, Jim Bell/Gerald Glanville Collection.

Monickers

The "Monicker", as it was used in Silverton, was not a term of derision. It was an earned title, linking the bearer with his exploits or disaster. Men remember a monicker long after a proper name has grown dim in their memories.

The San Juan had its share of these colorful characters. They were neither Saints nor Sinners, and they had a zest for life, each in his own way. Often they came by their nicknames by accident as well as talent. In recalling some of them, it's not my intent to embarrass any who may still be with us or belittle the memory of those who have departed. And should this happen, I offer my sincere apology.

No muster of their names could pass up "The Wooden Man". Both of Patty's legs and an arm had been burned away when a powerline's high voltage went to the ground through his body. So they made him some wooden ones and gave him a poolroom and bowling alley up over Billy Cole's store.

"Christmas Tree John"- The way it was, his party got a little out of hand, and John used his Christmas tree as a convincer to bring the gathering back to order.

"High Pockets"- A despondent philosopher who rode a fifty pound box of dynamite across the bar. No funeral rites were necessary.

"Slippery Tom"- Slippery spent his days at the deal table, an honest man. But then you sat in a game at your own risk, no matter where you played.

"Lion Tamer"- He came to town with a dog and pony show and decided to stay. At first, he wasn't able to leave.

"Boxcar Kelly"- When he ran out of money a boxcar was good enough, and all were welcome to share it with him.

"Shamrock"- Among his many accomplishments was his ability as a waiter. He was an artist at his work and could make hamburger seem like the finest filet mignon the house could serve.

"Caby, the Bellhop"- Caby had trained for the opera in England but liked the job as night-clerk at the hotel better.

"Big and Little Chip"- Brothers who worked as dealers at the various temples of chance. They were upstanding gentlemen and ran square games, and they had the town's respect.

"Tennessee"- Personification of the freedom-loving breed that hails from that state. Fear was something far beyond his comprehension. He walked up to the muzzle of a double-barrel shotgun in the hands of a crazed drunk and disarmed the fool.

45

"Shorty Mink", whose real name was Henry Meinke, spent his life as an assistant to the doctor at the Sunnyside Mine. He is pictured here retired at his home on Snowden Street. Ray Doud Photo/Jim Bell Collection, San Juan County Historical Society.

"Badger Bill"- Refereed the greatest Badger Fight ever held in the old Town of Eureka. And so earned his title.

"Twice Tason"- Some wit coined the monicker out of his name (John Johnson) and it stuck to him like a two cent postage stamp. Twice Tason didn't care about working for wages. But each spring after a winter on some prospect hole he'd taken a fancy to, a carload of good crude ore was usually ready for the smelter. He spent the summers enjoying Silverton's night life, with a pocket full of silver dollars, and a half yard of gold chain across his vest with a quarter-pound watch hung on the end of it.

Picturesque? Yes, I think they were. About the only place their proper names ever appeared was on the voting register. At times, it was hinted by defeated candidates that, although the gentlemen had long since cashed in their chips, some of them were still voting a straight ticket.

That's the kind of bulldog stubbornness it took to whittle a living out of the San Juan's granite.

Winning a Monicker

Aany sport or excitement to liven up an existence as close to hibernation as a winter in the San Juan was more than welcome. A group of stalwarts who headquartered at Eureka were capable of some pretty weird innovations.

Bill, one of their number and a late-comer to the mill's work force, was very much a man of the big outside world. His expertise and knowledge on all matters concerning sports and entertainment was phenomenal, and he never lost an opportunity to impress the boys with this fact. At times, his condescension and patronage were a little more than the fellows could take.

Mac's Poolhall was home-base for these "freewheelers," and they were inclined to the more robust types of entertainment. They were responsible for a brutally cruel pas-time of pitting a fighting dog against a savage wild badger in mortal combat. The sheriff, as well as several civic organizations, were trying to stamp out the cruel sport. But re-gardless of the law's efforts, a successful fight or two would be pulled off each winter. The fact that Eureka boasted no resident lawman made the place an ideal locale from the promoters' point of view.

As it happened, the news came down from the mine by word of mouth, very qui-etly. A real man-sized badger had been caught, and the boys were looking for a fight, that is if the mill bunch could dig up a dog good enough to bet their money on. All they had to do was send the word up, and the mine gang would be glad to bring their animal down and have a go at it. Of course, it would have to be a night when the sheriff couldn't make it up from the county seat at Silverton. But, if he did, all bets were off.

Some of the boys leaked the gossip to Bill confidentially and asked his advice. He was all for it. Bill bragged (and no one could prove otherwise) that he'd raised and trained the best badger-fighting dogs east of the Mississippi River. That statement made quite an impression on the mill bunch. They asked Bill if he would consider serving as the referee, if they decided to accept the challenge from the mine.

The request flattered the little guy. And he stated for the benefit of the committee and his poolhall-cronies that his decisions as a badger fight referee had never been ques-tioned in the whole state of Missouri. So word was sent to the mine: When conditions permitted, they could bring their fighting animal down, leave their money, and take the bloody carcass back with them after the fight. Not only did the mill bunch have a good dog, but an experienced referee as well.

The January weather cooperated. A storm had blocked the road to the county seat, and the word went out on the grapevine. By nine o'clock that evening, every man who could slip out his back door without his wife collaring him had sneaked into the dark clubhouse. Not a light was visible anywhere in the building. A casual observer would have sworn the mining camp had gone to bed as it usually did on a cold winter night. The poolhall bunch had disappeared, too. Old Mac sat in his chair by the stove, staring glumly at his front door and silent cash register.

Inside the clubhouse, all windows had been tightly covered. The only light was a single, shaded bulb hanging low, illuminating a fifteen foot circle in the middle of the dance floor. Although everything was innocently quiet outside, all hell was loose in the clubhouse. Committeemen were valiantly trying to select officials acceptable to both sides. Fistfights broke out and had to be quelled. The betting odds changed as opinions on the fighting qualities of both animals were argued back and forth. The evening might well have ended up in a free-for-all between the factions. Finally, a compromise was reached. Three men from the mine would act as handlers for the badger, and three from the mill for the dog. After some argument over Bill's qualifications as a referee, both sides agreed to let him officiate.

The rules for the contest were then recited for everyone's benefit. As required, a suitable rope had been attached to the badger's collar. The referee's duty would be to keep the fighting animals within the lighted circle by limiting the amount of slack in the tether rope. The dog would be free of any restraint and wear a studded fighting collar to give his throat some protection. The committee had provided suitable clothing for the referee, and would he please get ready. It was long past time for the fight to start.

So far, Bill had stood up under the strain very well. But the excitement and action was pretty heady stuff. He was at a point where he reacted to the committee's instructions automatically. They put a pair of heavy white rubber mill shoes on his feet, a pair of baseball shinguards on his legs, a catcher's belly protector around his middle, and a wire mask over his face. Then, they topped him off with a miner's safety cap with the bill turned back over his neck and finished the ensemble with a heavy yellow shaft slicker and elbow-length welder's gloves. Once they had Bill encased in his protective armor, they stationed him at one side of the lighted circle and gave him his final instructions.

According to the rules, as soon as the badger was brought in, one of the handlers would turn the loose end of the tether rope over to Bill. Then, at the count of three, a starting gun would be fired. He was to yank the badger out onto the floor. At the same time, the dog would be released. From then on, it was up to Bill to protect the patrons and himself as best he could. But at no time was he to permit the fighting animals beyond the circle of light.

Two men from the mine brought the badger in, inside a large barrel. They carried it horizontally with a heavy piece of burlap draped over the open end. The third man held the tether rope coiled in his hand, one end of it disappearing behind the burlap curtain. With his other hand, he rapped smartly on the burlap with a stick to keep the badger back in the barrel. When they had the barrel set to everyone's satisfaction, he uncoiled the rope with great care and gave its end to Bill.

The dog handlers were having trouble with "Old Dusty." The dog was a veteran of many a badger fight and shenanigan pulled by his poolhall pals. When he saw the badger barrel, he went berserk. But his handlers controlled him until a judge could count to three and fire the starting gun.

Bill, almost petrified with fear and excitement, managed to give the rope a lusty yank. But no vicious wild animal came charging out of that barrel. No snarling dog leaped to close with the badger in mortal combat. Only an old "Gray Graniteware Thundermug" was tied to the rope end and came clattering out on the floor. A roar of laughter burst from the crowd, and the house lights came on bright. Old Dusty sat on his haunches, tongue lolling out. If a dog can laugh, Old Dusty was laughing. He was the biggest ham in town.

Bill made a pathetic picture standing in the middle of the dance floor in his outlandish garb, holding a rope tied to an old thundermug. For a few moments, he seemed stunned. All around him, men were hooting and laughing at him but Bill was a real trooper. He bowed to his audience several times, and held up a hand for silence.

"Gentlemen," he said. "I have reached a decision. The badger won!"

He held the battered old pot above his head in the victory salute. From that instant, he was "Badger Bill" to everyone. And woe to the man who refused that night to drink beer from Bill's old thundermug.

Monikers are not bestowed lightly. Few men measure up to that something extra that's necessary to earn one. Bill was proud of his, and he had paid dearly for it. The poolhall bunch never groused about his tall yarns again, either. Some of them just might have been true.

John McNamara (on the left) as a little guy, was born in Eureka in 1917. He was there at the badger fights and even fought his friend Bob Gooch in the ring in a preliminary fight prior to the prize fight, prior to the badger fight. John McNamara Collection.

John McNamara, young John's grandfather, with John's aunt, Eileen McNamara, standing in front of the pool hall in Eureka in 1925. John McNamara Collection.

El Rio de las Animas Perdidas

reacher found him early one morning before daybreak, when he went out to empty the garbage from the hotel kitchen. Some meat scraps were still in a tin plate where the night chef usually fed him. He was dead, stretched out beside the trash barrels. In the half light of the alley lamp, Preacher could see that a little blood had seeped from the nose, and the eyes were glazed. "Dog" had run out his string and hung up his cue.

The old man knelt down to place a hand on Dog's head. It felt cold. He sat back on his heels, head bowed, his hand on the furry shoulder. Dog had been about the only friend he had. After a bit, he got stiffly to his feet and shuffled back into the hotel to finish cleaning up the kitchen. Pat, the night cop, had come in and was helping himself to a cup of coffee at the urn. So Preacher told him Dog had died and was lying out back in the alley.

"That's too bad, old man," Pat said. "I'll leave word at Town Hall. The street gang can pick up the carcass and take it to the dump. Anyway, we didn't have to shoot him, Preacher. I didn't think he'd make it through the winter, but he did. Well, it's better this way. Guess you'll miss him, eh?"

Preacher and Dog had a lot in common. Both were bums. Nobody knew where they came from, and no one cared. Although the wizened little man was a whiskey-soak, he'd earned the name of Preacher. He had a habit of blessing anyone who bought him a drink. In a way, he might have been mistaken for a clergyman who had seen better days. The frock coat, black hat, and collarless shirt he wore would give that impression. For the most part, people paid scant attention to him, disliking the whining voice and pale, watery eyes that shed tears of joy and self-pity over the occasional glass of whiskey that came his way. He and Dog had made a niche for themselves, working the saloons and dance halls.

Preacher mopped the kitchens, cleaned cuspidors, and swamped out after the last drunk staggered through the door into the street. Dog worked the alleys behind restaurants and cafes. Although he was a stray mongrel, he'd made friends in high places, such as with dish washers and the night shift cooks. He made out well enough bunking in a shack with Preacher. When it came time for a new license tag, Police Chief Sullivan put out the word and, a few bucks would show up from here and there. When he'd collected the right amount, he'd have a tag made out for Dog and put it in a desk drawer for safe keeping. Like Preacher, Dog didn't wear a collar either.

The word circulated that Dog had died. A few of the ladies and barflies of the redlight district gathered at Big Sally's for a drink or two in remembrance of old Dog. Preacher reached his limit early, and they laid him out in a back room to recover. By noon, the party had taken on the aspects of a full-scale wake. Trouble was, the body of the deceased was someplace down in the city dump.

All agreed it was an insult to an old friend's memory.

Sally was in the habit of issuing orders and having them obeyed. Three hundred pounds of bone and not so much fat is a convincing prerequisite for managing a dance hall and its clientele.

"Some of you boys go down and find that old animal," she said. "We'll give Dog a decent burial. Now hurry up. We don't have all day."

Chief Sullivan heard of the funeral plans and notified Sally that the dog would have to be taken outside the city limits for burial.

"Why don't we take him across the river and bury him?" she asked. "That's far enough out of town, and it should keep our lawman happy."

Long before the sun went down, all arrangements were complete. Dog's body was wrapped in an old blanket and placed on a two-wheeled cart somebody had borrowed from the livery stable. Lacking a floral offering, Sally substituted a well-stocked liquor hamper. The bottles made a pleasant tinkling sound as the cart rolled along, with no lack of willing hands to help with the pulling.

A number of the town's more wayward citizens joined the cortege as it moved up Blair Street toward a footbridge across the Animas River. A dog burial was a novelty and created some interest. The bottles in the hamper received a great deal of attention, too. In fact, the mourners were in quite a hilarious mood by the time they arrived at the river bank.

But the footbridge proved to be a problem. It was only two logs wide, with a two-by-twelve plank nailed lengthwise on top—and no hand rail. Even a sober man might hesitate to walk upright across the contraption. However, the mourners crossed one or two at a time. The braver ones walked boldly to prove they could hold their liquor. Some of the ladies weakened a little at midstream and went down on all fours to finish the crossing on their hands and knees. They had to tuck their skirts up about their waists in order to crawl. This maneuver met with hearty approval and brought forth some cryptic remarks that were a bit less than complimentary.

Preacher had sobered up enough to walk across under his own steam. But there was never an instant when he wasn't in danger of pitching headlong into the water. Finally, everybody was on the other side except Big Sally and the two men in charge of the cart.

"All right, you jockos," Sally yelled. "Pick up the old dog and carry him over. You can't pull the damn cart across a footlog."

After some cussing and grumbling, the two men found a way to suspend the carcass between them. With Sally right behind, they started across. Perhaps if she hadn't been so close, they might have made it. But the bridge timbers were old. Two men, a dead dog and three hundred pounds of woman were just too much weight at one time. The bridge broke in a splintering crash, dropping the men with their burden and Sally into four feet of icy water.

For a few seconds, the crowd was stunned to silence by the accident. Then, shouting with laughter, they offered suggestions on how best to get ashore, while they watched Sally and the men flounder about in the river. Sally grabbed a man's arm in each hand and hauled them back up on their feet.

"Come on, you guys, climb out on the bank with me," she yelled. "You can't swim in this ditch; there ain't enough water. When I find the clown that built that trap, I'll kill him."

She went splashing ashore, dragging a soaked man with each hand. Sally never needed help from anybody.

But the collapsing of the bridge brought the procession to a halt. Their guest of honor had disappeared. The corpse had been washed away down river.

A groan of despair went around when they realized Dog was gone. Near panic resulted when they discovered all the refreshments were still in the cart on the other side of the river, with no bridge for miles either up or down stream. Sally, as usual, pointed the way by voice and by action.

"Come on, you dance hall beauties and bar mechanics," she shouted. "The whiskey is on the other side of the river. A little water won't hurt those tender hides of yours."

She grabbed the two men she'd just floundered ashore with and plunged back in for a noisy, splashing crossing. Everyone followed Sally and her escorts into the water, while they shouted profanity and vulgar comments. The women were holding their skirts high to try and keep them dry, if they could. It had taken some time for the company to work their way over the footbridge but getting back to the hamper of bottles without a bridge took no time at all. Fording a cold mountain stream is something that's done speedily.

Preacher was reluctant to wade across with the others. None of the noisy crowd paid any attention to him. They gathered around the cart and passed the bottles until all were well fortified against pneumonia or a possible chill. Then they trooped off down town without a thought for the forlorn little man marooned on the other bank. He made a pathetic picture standing by the river in his long black coat and outlandish hat.

Finally, in desperation, he chose a spot where the water seemed more shallow and waded in. At midstream, he became excited and frightened. The water was icy cold, the current so swift he could hardly hold his footing against it. For a few minutes, he fought the river, then in a panic, attempted to dash the last steps to safety. He slipped, falling into a deeper run of the channel, and went under. Twice, he almost gained his feet again, but the long coat wrapped about his legs and dragged him down. A hand reached skyward for an instant, and vanished.

El Rio de las Animas Perdidas—the river of lost souls—had claimed its own.

Later that evening, the night cop dropped in at the cafe for a cup of coffee. The cook wanted to know if he'd seen Preacher anywhere on the street.

"Damn it, Pat," he said. "I can never find the bum when I need him. If you see the old fool, tell him to come in. I've a good notion to plant a boot on his butt. Don't tell him I said that, Pat, or he'll never show up."

"Some of the girls and gents buried Preacher's old dog this afternoon, George, or they tried to. I hear they got a little drunk and lost the carcass in the river. Could be Preacher had a bit too much and fell in, too. I'll see if he's around somewhere."

"Hell, Pat, I didn't know Preacher's old dog had died. I'm sorry to hear that. Well, I guess I'll have to go easy on him if he comes in tonight. You know, Pat, sometimes I half like the old devil."

Harry

He never seemed to change much. Kind of like an old fence—if a picket or two falls off nobody notices. I can't recall ever seeing him dressed in anything other than a blue-serge cap, dark shirt, paint-spattered pants and vest. He worked out of a local hardware store, as a plumber, tinner, and man of all trades.

It was only when some of our good townspeople were in trouble, or had a dirty job, that they remembered Harry. He replaced their broken windows, fixed their leaky water pipes, put the new stove grates in for them and took the stoppage out of the bathroom seat after Junior had plugged it up. Whatever had to be done, he could manage.

A few beers or a pint of wine on Saturday evening was about the extent of his social life. None of it ever showed in his behavior. The smile and kindly eyes squinting from under his cap bill were always the same. Along with his Cockney accent, shuffling walk and hunched shoulders he seemed as durable as an old pine-knot.

In the fall of 1918 the flu struck our town. For a while people fought the plague with spirit and courage. But their defenses crumbled as the death toll mounted. A time came when the dead could no longer be cared for in the usual manner. No help was available from other communities. They, like Silverton, were prostrate. Prepared food for those who could no longer care for themselves arrived by train daily. The Town Hall became a hospital, or, more aptly, a place to die. It seemed the black crepe of death was hung on every door in town.

Harry forsook his little shop behind the hardware store. Through those dark days he labored around the clock in the morgue. After the supply of coffins was exhausted, he made rough boxes for the dead or wrapped them in blankets as best he could before they were taken to the cemetery.

If he felt fear of the plague, he mastered it and lived with the dead. As long as there was a body to be cared for, he stayed at his self-imposed duty. His only rest was a short nap in a chair until called again to help a stricken family care for their dead.

Harry never wore a flu-mask, nor took any other precautions to protect himself against the infection. He was far too busy helping desperate people through their days of despair. If he wasn't needed at the morgue, he went to homes where families were down and helpless. Many a one walked the streets again because of him.

When it was all over, and the town had shaken off its terror after that winter of flu, Harry was back at work. He went shuffling along with a window pane, a rubber sewer-pump or a Stillson wrench tucked under his arm. Things were getting back to the way they should be, and no one doubted that Harry would be there to do the patching and fixing.

How do you measure the worth of a man? Is it by the castle he builds? By the battles he fights? Or perhaps by the wealth he amasses? I don't know, but I think the rod would have to be long to measure a little guy who stood tall and said to his neighbors, "Come, let me lend you a hand."

The Silverton cemetery in 1993. John Marshall Photo.

George's Bean Boiler

It didn't happen often, but every once in a while George would fire up his old bean boiler. Then he'd invite the whole mill crew in to eat with him. So, along with the other sawmill savages, I tramped up to the cookhouse. The rough board shack did for an office and warehouse as well. Word had gone around that the boss was having beans and ham for lunch. I was told to forget my lunch kit: it was eat with the boss or else.

At meal time, the wash-up procedure is about the same in all fly-by-night sawmills. You wait your turn for a dipper of cold water in a tin basin just outside the door. If there's a towel, you're lucky. If not, you use your own shirt tail to dry your hands and face.

Inside, George sat reading a paperback. He was altogether the logger, complete with a brown and red plaid shirt, spiked boots, and a battered hat. And no stranger had to be told the little guy was the boss. After four hours of hard work in the fresh air of the pine country, a man needs a good meal and a little rest. I had no idea what kind of cook he was, and I began to look for a way to slip out and get my lunch box. But there wasn't a chance with him sitting in his office by the door, almost like a guard.

Over close to one wall of this catchall room stood a wood-burning cook stove, and in the center, a plank table and two benches. Above the stove suspended on wires from the open rafters hung a large sign. It read: "Not necessarily approved by Duncan Hines."

That's about all there was to the cook house, except for the copper boiler on the stove. It was the kind women used at one time to boil clothes. A wire hook had been fastened to the front handle of the thing, and a graniteware dipper hung from it. Of course, there was a coffee pot, too. No attempt had been made to set the table. On the end closest to the door stood a stack of one and a half quart serving bowls, some coffee cups, and a pan with soup spoons.

By the time I'd overcome a little of my disappointment in the setup, I was in the chow line with a bowl in my hand. I reached into the copper kettle for some beans—or whatever was in the damned thing. The smell was sure good, and I began to take an interest in it.

A few of the more important members of the crew sat at the table. The rest of us found packing cases or whatever was handy to sit on. The odor of good hot food is a bit more than just pleasure, it's a promise, and your anticipation runs high. I dipped in my spoon and tried a mouthful. Man, I'd struck pure gold. One of the most pleasant things in life is finding good food in unsuspected places.

By nosing about a little, I learned something of the workings of George's bean boiler. Everything he used was the best that could be had, regardless of price. The pinto beans were fresh crop, and field dried. I don't think there was a bean in my bowl with the skin broken, just big and tender and good. Small bite-sized onions and potato chunks and plenty of premium ham made up the rest of the ingredients. George's secret was the cooking time of each. Nothing was over-cooked or under-cooked. There was no hint of a sticky puree; just a clear consomme gravy with a fine bead of richness. The old man had a gourmet touch.

A gentleman heads out to seek adventure in the high country—probably in 1900. Maybe he had just got some good bargains at the nickel counter. Ray Doud Photo, Jim Bell/Gerald Glanville Collection.

Louis tries his luck at Emerald Lake. The Wyman Collection.

Poco Loco

Louie and I were getting an outfit together for a more rugged than usual fishing expedition into the upper reaches of the Pine River drainage (Southwestern Colorado), to remote Emerald Lake in particular.

We had to shake our outfit down so it would fit on one pack mule and two saddle animals. Riding along the Continental Divide for twenty miles or more, most of it above timber line, we had to leave the more plush accouterments behind. It took considerable arguing and profanity. But we wound up with the bare essentials: a metal tackle box filled with Louie's trout killing gadgetry and not much else.

In his mesmerized state of mind as a novice trout-fly-tier and lure inventor, Louie was sure he'd created the wonder trout catcher of all time. The genius had rigged up a long watertight wooden trough with a glass window fitted in the bottom of it. We set the thing up level on two sawhorses and filled it about three-quarters full with water. All spring and early summer I spent hours and hours dragging the silly monstrosities he'd dreamed up back and forth through the water in the tank. Each lure had to be tied to a short piece of fish line. All the while friend Louie lay flat on his back beneath the contraption gazing up through the window at the performance of his pretty mechanical bugs. Making the things operate to his satisfaction was next to impossible. How his point of view could fathom a fish's intuition was beyond me.

The trip was a mighty effort on our part to get into the back country, away from the litter of bread wrappers, empty bean cans, and fished out trout water.

We'd brought along a small tent, because timber line spruce trees don't provide much protection at night. Louie insisted on two frying pans, too. He said that was so we could cook a well balanced meal of fried trout and flapjacks, providing of course we caught some fish.

We did. The lake was home to lots of big Rainbow Trout. They were savage as hungry mountain horseflies, and willing to fight it out with any fool fisherman who dared to throw a man-made lure into their lake. For a time we carried on an all-out war with them. Louie caught fish with his creations that, up to that time, had never produced anything but a ripple on either a lake or stream.

He was happy, but I get bored and restless fishing in one place from a lake shore and strolled off searching for the inlet to the lake. The promise and challenge of a beautiful clear mountain trout stream is irresistible to me. I wanted a chance to set my hooks in a big fellow that would top anything Louie could come up with. The stream, when I found it, had lost its way and was wandering around in some old beaver ponds.

Big trout and beaver ponds go together, so I moved up carefully for a look see. They were there, several of them, well out of casting reach. The only way to get close enough was to wade out into the pond. Slowly and quietly I waded along in icy, crystal clear water just a little over knee-deep. I noticed an abandoned beaver burrow on the bottom, but promptly forgot it in my impatience to cast a fly nearer those big ones.

The combination I like best, when trout are taking wet flies, is a Royal Coachman on the dropper loop of a leader and trailing a Ginger Quill. This rig will take fish in fly season when nothing else will. The first few casts produced a pan size "Brooky." He was nothing but an upstart; back to the pond he went. Then I laid the flies out nicely a bit nearer the big fish. Almost at the end of my retrieve one struck the Coachman. He couldn't have taken me at a greater disadvantage, with yards of slack line and only limited space to maneuver in. Big trout choose the battlefield, not the fisherman.

Finally my line snarled until it was impossible to reel it in or play it out. The fish had me fighting with my back to the bank. Bad as it was, the situation worsened. A second leviathan struck the Ginger Quill, and I had two big bolts of red and silver lightning tied to a fragile fly rod by a three pound test leader and a messed up line. The battle ended the only way it could. Both fish broke loose, threw the hooks, and went elsewhere. A beaver pond is a hell of a place to fish. Well, anyway, I had a tale that would top anything Louie might think up.

Sadly I turned to wade ashore and stepped right into the damned beaver burrow; liquid ice six feet deep. Even on a warm August day, water in a timber line beaver pond is the coldest fluid on earth. When it runs in over the tops of your waders it's a chilling experience. When it comes up to your belt buckle it's a disaster. But when your ears submerge and your hat floats off it's overwhelming. I didn't climb out of the burrow, I rocketed out and went for shore so fast I think I ran on the surface, and promised myself I'd never fish in a beaver pond again.

A stripper act wasn't popular at that time. But I did one, without the benefit of an audience, wrung out my clothes and hung them on the willows to dry. Then I started a fire. Matches and a piece of candle in a waterproof container are a must in the high country. Right then I wouldn't have traded my little packet for anything I owned. My smudge of willow sticks and beaver cuttings put out more smoke than heat. I was about to pull on my boots and head for camp when friend Louie showed up.

He can be the most aggravating guy, and he can do it without saying a word. Nothing seems to surprise him. A mean gleam came into his eyes when he saw me dancing around my fire naked, swatting flies and mosquitoes, while I tried to keep from freezing to death. The grin on his face spread, and the more it spread the less I liked it.

"What you been doing? Go for a swim? Or did you fall in?"

"I tried to jump across the pond but it was too far. What the hell do you think I tried to do?"

He took off his coat and shirt, then put his coat back on again and handed me the shirt.

"Here," he said. "I can get along without the shirt but I'll be damned if I'll let you wet my pants. Your old man should have broken you of that habit years ago, Boy! You need some more training."

By that time my teeth were chattering so bad I couldn't talk, I just pointed to the beaver pond. He thought I meant for him to try his luck on the lunkers lurking over near the other side. But I was trying to warn him about the beaver burrow in the bottom. He didn't know it was there and couldn't see it because of the patch of muddy water where I'd floundered around getting out. It was a nice gesture of gratitude on my part for the loan of his shirt. But the wise guy paid no attention to my stuttering.

"Ok, ok, don't get excited," he said. "I'll give it a try. Is there a particular trout in the pond you'd like for dinner, Sir?"

It's a real pleasure to watch an expert cast. The flies settle on the surface with scarcely a ripple, almost as lifelike as the real thing. He took several nice trout and kept only one or two. In the taking he stepped across the beaver hole from side to side, time after time. How a man could move about in that puddle of muddy water, catching fish, and not fall into the burrow was just plain fisherman's luck.

I waited on the bank shivering in Louie's shirt and not much else. It would be fun to see how my smart-aleck "Pardner" handled the situation if his hat floated off like mine had. I needed the last laugh to even up the score. He never stepped into the hole. He knew what had happened to me and wasn't about to make a fool of himself by doing the same thing. Finally I gave up and headed for camp, the cold was too much.

Later that evening while we loafed around the fire, and I was warm and dry again, friend Louie had to get in a bit of ribbing.

"How big was the one that got away?"

"It wasn't one. It was two, both on at the same time."

"Well I guess you might handle one all right, but two? Oh no! I think you'd better fish with only one fly, it's safer. How many times did they tow you back and forth across the pond?"

"They didn't tow me any place. They pulled me under."

"Yeah, that's a pretty big story. At least it's bigger than the fish you caught. But I think a guy who chases a trout down a beaver burrow and then dives in to try and catch it, well he has to be poco loco."

"I know, I know! It's the only way a fisherman can survive."

Back in camp, Louis knew our luck had been pretty good, but maybe he should've brought a bigger frying pan. The Wyman Collection.

The Sellout

About the time hunting season opens, big game hunters become quite erratic. They're subject to fantastic flights of imagination. Their dreams are so real to them, they can't tell fact from fancy. They'll go to great lengths to help out a fellow nimrod. Then for the very devilment of it, they'll suddenly turn and deftly sell him out. Often their pranks are so smoothly engineered that the victim is unaware he's been had. Finesse is a virtue sportsmen regard highly.

Two of Silverton's active devotees of the art lived across the alley from each other in the same block, which is a very handy arrangement during the preparation and assembly of equipment for a big game hunting trip. Their back-yards became staging areas; jammed with trucks, horse-trailers, and, as time ran out, horses too. The neighbors endured the confusion each season in numb silence.

Oddly enough, the two didn't hunt together. Louie, always the perfectionist, joined a column that moved out well before opening day. They campaigned in the Crested Butte area, in the Gunnison National Forest. The expeditions were planned right down to the smallest detail, and usually he brought home meat to hang on his ridge-pole.

Jake planned everything too but never could get around to using his plan. He'd work until midnight the day before the season, getting ready. Then he'd pile out at 2:00 a.m. to load his horses and gear, and take off for some place he hadn't intended to go at all. His hunting range extended from the Rio Grande Pyramid to the LaPlata Mountains. And he was a fairly successful hunter. Perhaps he and Louie remained friends because they were never in camp together.

But one year Louie failed to make a kill and fill his license. Of course Jake was lucky and had a bull elk, big as a horse, hanging in his garage. He gave Louie a terrible ribbing about his hunting ability, and all Louie could do was grin and bear it.

A bull elk that has been running with the herd is a tough customer, either afield or on the dinner table. After Jake had taken care of the gratuities around the neighborhood, he still had a lot of elk meat that resembled a fair grade of boot leather.

Jake discussed the problem with his pal, and a solution was forthcoming immediately. "Make corned elk out of it," Louie said, "and you'll have the best salt meat you ever ate." So in due time the meat was put down in the corning brine. Louie supervised the corning process, while Jake paid the bill for supplies.

Corning meat is a time-consuming procedure, and Jake wasn't a patient man. Long before the meat had time to cure, he fished a piece out of the barrel and tried it. But his family turned thumbs down. Finally he told Louie they'd have to haul it off to the dump. Nobody could eat it. It was just no good.

Louie had a solution for that problem, too.

"Just leave it there," he said. "I can feed it to my dogs. They'll get rid of it for you."

Jake didn't like the idea too well, but as long as he couldn't use the meat the dogs might as well have it. And so the matter rested until spring when he happened to look in the barrel and found there was still meat in it. He made a fast trip across the alley and told Louie to hurry up and feed the last of the meat—he was tired of having the stuff around.

"Hell, man," Louie said, "I'm not feeding that meat to the dogs. That's the best corned meat we've ever eaten. Why don't you folks try some of it?"

"You mean you've been eating my corned elk meat all winter? And not feeding it to your damned dogs? And it's good meat?"

"That's right, you told me you didn't like it, and it was no good, remember? But man, it sure is."

Hunters are like that. If one plays the sucker, it's just his hard luck—sympathy is something he won't get. A few days later when Louie went over to Jake's for a piece of meat, there was a big padlock on the door. He saw Jake glaring at him from a kitchen window, and for a while there was a little tension between the two.

But by the time trout season opened, expeditions were moving out and returning with their usual frequency. It's hard to sit down to a bang-up meal with the guy from across the alley and still stay mad at him. Even if he did slicker you out of half your elk meat.

Louis thinks it's fair game. The Wyman Collection.

The Schoolmarm

Once upon a time there lived a happy and prosperous people in a small mining camp called Eureka. Most every year a new school teacher came to preside over their one-room school house. Her coming was an event scrutinized from every angle by the village Dandies. And if she happened to be "Pretty, Witty and Gay" (as the old song has it), the rivalry for her smile became real hot. Kind of like "Pistolas" at ten paces.

Pete, a pace-setter among the Beau Brummells who parked their cars in front of Mac's Poolroom, invited a few of his pals over to his shack for a consultation concerning the new teacher. She would be arriving soon, and he suggested that they ought to select one gent to act as her escort. The question was how to make a fair choice?

Things really warmed up at the meeting. Everyone had a different notion on how to do it. Some agreed one thing and some another. Buzz, who never agreed with anybody, said, "Cut the cards and be done with the silly business."

Pete was for doing the sporting thing, and help out whoever was chosen with a little financial aid, too. So he thought the only way to settle it was a freeze-out game of poker. Each man who cared to could sit in for a twenty dollar stack. The winner take all and the lady. His idea met with instant approval, and the game was on.

In the early hours of the morning, Pete and Buzz, the last two die-hards, faced each other across the table with their stakes in the game about even. Buzz wanted to deal one more round, let the winner take all, and call it quits. Pete agreed and drew the winning hand.

Although the game had been very hush-hush, word got around (there were leaks then, too), and someone notified the lady of the situation and assured her she might be embarrassed upon her arrival by certain rather wild young men of the community. All of which the conspirators were unaware of. However, it turned out that "Miss Mary"—as we shall call the lady—was a gal of spirit, and she thought she'd like to meet the gentleman who'd won the right to be her escort in a poker game.

Silverton boasted a daily passenger train arriving at nine o'clock each evening. Of course Pete was on hand to meet it and drive the new school teacher on to Eureka. When the conductor helped Miss Mary down from the chaircar vestibule, Pete knew he'd hit the jackpot. Miss Mary was all a young lady should be, all done up in a neat, stylish outfit. He introduced himself and explained he was to meet her train and drive her on to Eureka but thought she might like to stop at the hotel for a late dinner first.

Pete was about to help her into his car, but she hesitated, turned and smiled at him, and said, "Sir, I would like to know—and I'm sure you'll tell me—what was the winning hand?"

He was speechless for a moment, and that happened very seldom indeed. But Pete was a true cavalier. He swept off his hat and bowed. "Miss Mary," he said, "I filled my hand with the Queen of Hearts."

She laughed with delight at his answer, and said, "It will be fun to have a late dinner at the hotel."

For a time, the village Dandies envied Pete and his luck. He squired the new schoolmarm at parties and at dances, and his shiny black coupe had to be polished every time it rolled out of the garage. And his sour-faced poker pals were footing the bills.

But things began to change, and Miss Mary was seen quite often accompanied by a gentleman whose position in the community was substantial. By the time the New Year revel came around, Pete was spending his evenings at the pool hall again—with his old cronies. While there were some broad hints, nobody wanted to ask him outright: How come he'd lost out? But the last hand in the freezeout game still rankled Buzz, and he told Pete it was his opinion that they'd sent a boy to market.

"Well, Buzz," Pete said, "it's darned hard to beat an Ace High Diamond Flush."

Her name is lost in time but she was definately a schoolmarm. San Juan County Historical Society.

The Happening

Working a lease on a mine in the San Juan is at best a precarious occupation. When an unexpected event occurs to add complications, the results are often ludicrous. Things can even become a bit violent.

It happened that way the summer Charley, Lud, and I worked a sub-lease on the San Antone Mine on Red Mountain.

It was all hand work—no compressor, and the hoist and pumps were steam-driven. We had no money to buy fuel for the boiler, and darned little for anything else. So we burned everything we could lay our hands on to make steam. It takes a fabulous amount of firewood to keep a fifty-horse boiler working at a hundred pounds pressure.

Lud skidded in every dead stick of timber he could find on the mountain side, and it kept him and a team of horses busy most of the time. We cut the logs into five foot lengths to fit the boiler firebox. The larger lengths had to be split in quarters as well, and that job fell to me. One day, I'd work underground ten hours, the next day cut boiler firewood for twelve hours and help out with the drill sharpening between times.

It was on this wood cutting detail that I ran into trouble. Lud had skidded a large log into the wood yard close behind the shaft-house. Those big pieces of timber were too hard to split with wedges and a maul. So I'd bore a hole in them with a ship auger, load it with a half-stick of dynamite, and split the log by blasting. It worked real well, and I could pile up a good big stack of boiler fuel in a short while.

But that big log gave the hoistman and me a bad time. I started working it up in the usual way, just one blast at a time as I needed it. But all I was getting was a few chips. The fuel pile was getting low, and the hoistman came out to see why the production had fallen off.

"Listen kid," he said. "If you'll use two holes in those big pieces, you might get something done. The way you're going at it, there won't be enough wood for coffee tonight, let alone keep a fire in the boiler."

One reason a youngster survives in a mine is the sage counseling of older and more experienced men. I didn't think much of the two-hole deal. It seemed to me it would be better to drill a hole deeper, and use more powder—and make one blast do the work. But I drilled two holes, one in each end of the log as he instructed. Then I loaded each with a half-stick of dynamite, spit the fuses and ducked into the shaft-house for protection. I held up two fingers to indicate there were two shots to go. He nodded "OK," then set the hoist's hand-brake and settled back on his chair to wait.

Hoistmen usually built their own chairs to fit their own personal needs and comfort; the do-it-yourself creation he'd made was nailed securely to the wall back of the hoist. The first shot went as expected, and we waited for the second. But we didn't know the first shot had caused the log to roll down against the shaft-house. The second explosion came from right outside, behind the hoistman's chair. I think his reflexes had something to do with the action. But I can't deny that a half-stick of dynamite exploding against the wall transmitted a man-sized wallop to the seat of his pants—via the chair bottom.

He went right up into the air and cleared the hoist drum and landed on his feet running. He made it out to the waste dump before he could stop. There was quite a bulge in the wall, and his chair was tipped forward a little. It gave the impression it had just tossed its occupant out.

Then I did the wrong thing again. I saw him coming back into the building rubbing his backside, and I started to laugh. The next instant, he was after me with a length of oak tamping stick. What I saw in that man's eyes was pure murder.

We went around the wood yard and through the shafthouse a few times. But I figured I needed more running room, so I took off across the hillside hoping I'd find Lud before the guy broke my head with his oak stick. He gave up the chase after a short distance and went back to the mine.

I didn't think I should have been blamed for what had happened. It was his idea to use two shots in the big ones. Hoistmen are supposed to be men of great experience and know-how. I traded jobs with Lud for awhile, just to keep out of his way. Eventually, peace was restored but not on a very friendly basis.

Primo Segafredo runs the Washington Incline Hoist at the American Tunnel level almost 2000 feet below lake Emma in 1962. Zeke Zanoni Collection.

Spruce Tree Soup

I looked at my watch for the second time in fifteen minutes. Noon had come and gone, and I was hungry, and wanted my lunch. Up the slope a short way, where the cabin stood in a fringe of timberline spruce and juniper, Ludwig was supposed to be getting our lunch ready. He was the senior member of our three-way partnership. He did the cooking and camp chores, while Charley and I handled the heavy work running the drilling rig.

The old Snowflake mining claim we were prospecting lies just east of U.S. Highway No. 550 where it crosses the Red Mountain Divide in San Juan County, Colorado. Each sunrise of a new day brought the promise of a fortune awaiting us deep in the formation where the long drills searched and probed. Each sunset faded into weary disappointment. But we pressed our luck seeking the El Dorado every miner dreams of.

Lud (short for Ludwig) appeared in the cabin door carrying a large pressure-cooker. He had a gunny-sack wrapped around it, to keep from burning his hands. Lud always used a full-sized gunny-sack as a pot holder. If any of us noticed a bit of grit between our teeth at mealtime, it was best to ignore it, because the old man did a good job as camp cook.

Even though none of us had been to town in weeks for supplies, he would surprise us with a roast of mutton or a platter of fried chicken. Charley and I were very careful not to hurt his feelings by mentioning the bird shot that showed up in some of his best efforts. Lud had learned the fine art of foraging in the Italian Army. He said a good big tom cat was a welcome challenge to an army chef's artistry. I have always figured a person would be stupid indeed to question the source of a good meal. He could darn well end up by having to do the cooking himself.

Lud hastened to set his cooker on a bench beneath an old spruce tree beside the cabin. The bench was more table than bench and about the most used thing we had in camp. I answered his signal, to come and get it by closing the throttle on the drill-rig's engine.

"That time?" Charley asked as he looked up from his work.

"Yeah, Lud says come and get it. Man am I hungry."

While we were climbing the scant fifty yards to the cabin, Lud popped out of the door and yelled for us to hurry up. At times he mixed a good deal of his Italian with his English. The result never failed to be vivid, and his meaning remarkably clear. But it took some getting used to.

"Come on, you fellows. Good hell, you're slow. You run that machine like you come to eat—no wonder we don't make a dime. Tomorrow you cook the polenta, and maybe I come to eat when I'm damn good and ready."

"OK, Lud, OK. What's for lunch?" Charley's voice came from behind his noisy sputtering in the wash basin. I cocked an ear to hear Lud recite the menu for our benefit, hoping there might be a change from yesterday, and the day before that.

"I made soup, we only had a little meat left. You boys better make a strike soon or we don't eat. I go down to the sheep camp after bit. That Mexican boy's okay. He'll sell us a chunk of sheep. I get some."

I glanced at the gauge on the cooker as I went inside to sit down. It said fifteen pounds, pretty high, I thought, but then, Lud was doing the cooking. A moment later he opened a petcock to let the pressure drop so the old kettle could be opened. He was in a hurry and opened the valve wide. Charley and I sat inside at the table talking and waiting for our meal to be dished up.

It's nerve-racking to have a beautiful June day split in two right down the middle without warning. Lud's roar of anger and frightened disbelief did that and more. Charley and I made the door at the same instant, and there we jammed up with our backsides inside the cabin and our heads and shoulders outside. Our predicament was not important compared to the show Lud was putting on under the spruce tree. He had opened the cooker and was pointing at the empty pot while he danced around excitedly.

"Look you fellers!" he yelled. "It's gone, every damn thing. You tell me what happen? The whole damn soup is gone! Cristo Mio! She's a crazy thing."

At first it was hard to tell what he meant. Lud pranced about under the tree, peering into the empty cooker, first from one side and then the other. He kept rubbing the back of his neck, his face and forehead, while his Italian tongue crackled like a Chinese celebration. Then it dawned on Charley and me what had happened to Lud and his soup kettle. It was hard to believe, even though we had witnessed the event first-hand.

When Lud opened the petcock, the pressure had blown the foaming soup and meat through the port into the lower branches of the tree. The old pot had steamed itself completely dry, and a lot of it had condensed on the boughs and twigs just above him. A gentle rain of soup was falling on his head while he tried to solve the mystery. It trickled down the back of his neck, it soaked into his hair and ran down his nose to his mouth. In his excitement he didn't realize what was happening to him. Suddenly he stopped dead still and looked up into the tree. His mouth opened slowly and a little of the broth fell on his tongue. In utter disbelief he backed away, crossing himself and praying to his patron saint, all the while gazing at the tree in dumbfounded amazement.

Charley and I ducked back inside and lay in our bunks—convulsed with laughter, but not daring to make a sound. Finally I staggered over to the stove for a cup of coffee and some beans. Outside Lud was making a lot of noise washing up and putting things to rights. After a bit the camp settled down to a quietness almost beyond belief, so I looked out to see what came next. Lud was headed down country for the sheep camp.

"Would you like mutton chops for supper, Charley?" I asked.

"Well, sure, I like mutton chops. But right now I'll settle for a plate of those beans and a cup of coffee. And I'd like to make you a bet," he said. "I'll bet you a quart of good Scotch whiskey, (payable only if we make a strike) that Lud never uses his pressure cooker again."

I called his bet. The old man never used it again, and I never had to pay it off either.

The Old Man

Every resident mine manager is known as "the old man". Age has nothing to do with it. It's a title bestowed by the crew, whether they like him or not. It always carried a note of respect for his authority. His signature on the paycheck backs it up.

In the early days of the Shenandoah Mine, the machine shop crew at the mill became used to the old man coming and going through the shop. It was the shortest way between the mill and general offices. Often he'd stop and comment on whatever work was in progress. There was very little that went on about the plant and mine he wasn't well informed on.

Most of our side activities he chose to ignore, but when he found something he couldn't tolerate he'd come down hard on us. He was recognized throughout the Southwest as one of the best managers in the business. And on matters of policy most everyone figured he was reasonably fair.

The shop crew at the mill developed a little side line, a kind of good neighbor thing, that just seemed to have sprung up by itself. There was no money in it. The miners on their way to work in the morning would leave some household gadget in the shop to be mended. Then they'd pick it up after shift on their way home.

Quite often when we came to work we'd find a youngster's toy tucked away behind a tool box or under a work bench. Bicycles, tricycles, little red wagons, and even a little girl's doll buggy came our way. With each toy came a silent plea—"Please, mister, will you fix it for me?"

We had to keep the stuff out of sight as much as possible, even though we suspected the old man knew all about our side line. We watched his comings and goings, and when he went to the mine on inspection trips, we'd pull out our backlog of toys and try to get caught up with our work.

One day a new angle developed. I glanced up from my work and saw a woman standing in the doorway. She seemed unsure as to whether she should come in or not, so I went over to see if we could help her in some way. She said her husband worked at the mine. They thought if she brought their little boy's leg brace in, someone might be able to fix it for him. She handed me one of those monstrosities of bent iron and leather straps which doctors and technicians use to harness kids crippled from polio.

The shop crew got to know that brace and its owner, Tommy, quite well. He was a rough one, twelve years old, and he'd try anything. Though his leg must have given him real pain at times, I never heard him whimper. Bicycles, basketball, baseball or anything else where the action was fast, was just his meat.

Sometimes we almost gave up trying to keep him on two legs. It got so I thought leather and iron weren't strong enough to hold him. To Tommy, the world was a great big wonderful place to have fun in. And a leg brace—no handicap at all.

On one occasion he came limping into the shop, climbed up on the work bench, and informed me, "I broke it."

"So, what's new about that?"

"I fell off a burro. He was running fast. But I didn't hurt my other leg."

"Well, in that case we should be able to get you back on two legs again. What are you planning to do? Ride in the Labor Day Parade?"

It happened that the old man was on a trip to the mine and would be gone for a time, so we didn't have him to worry about. The shop welder mended the broken part for us. Then Tommy and I clamped it in the bench vise while we finished it off and fitted a new pin to the hinge joint.

For convenience sake, I kept Tommy perched up on a box on the work bench, so I could find him when the job was finished. He always gave me a run-down on important events and could ask questions about everything he saw in the shop and mill faster than I could answer them.

Suddenly he fell silent. I turned to see what had attracted his attention. The old man stood back of me, taking in the whole performance.

"Well," I thought, "Here we go, caught at the scene of the crime."

"Are you repairing the lad's leg brace?"

I told him I was and introduced Tommy. The old man shook hands with him and addressed him with the full title of "Mister". Tommy sat up straight on his box and grew an inch or two.

"Louis," the old man said, "Spare no effort. Do the very best job on that brace you can." Then he shook hands with Tommy, said good-bye, and went back to his office.

Yes, the old man was boss. He hired and fired, he carried the weight of responsibility for a big outfit on his shoulders. But he could still find time to be concerned about a little boy with his leg in a brace.

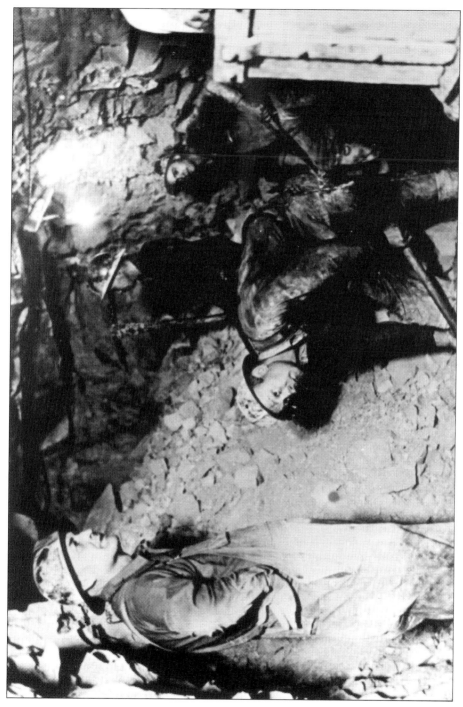

Four miners at work at the Midway Tunnel in the Sunnyside Mine, 1934. The shift boss, Gary Gardner, is at the left. James Hook Collection, San Juan County Historical Society.

Cool, Real Cool

Repairing and relining the primary crusher at the old Shenandoah Mine was always a knock-down-and-drag-out battle. It required all the mill and mine shop crews.

Half of them started the dismantling job at midnight after the evening shift had gone home. The other half came on at 8:00 a.m. the following morning to relieve them. And if we had the crusher back together again and running at the end of ten or twelve hours of back-breaking labor, we were lucky.

The entire crushing plant was housed underground in an old worked-out stope. Like all such installations, it was badly crowded. The lack of room to work and the compact arrangement of the equipment made repairs far more difficult than under normal conditions. When we had the crusher torn down and parts strewn all over every available square foot of floor space, I often thought: this is what the world would look like if it caved in.

Zincking in the liners fell to the day shift crew. That part of the job required 7 to 8 hundred pounds of molten zinc, and it all had to be ready to pour at one time. Usually we started the oil burning furnace under the big zinc pot when we came on shift in the morning. Melting that much slab zinc at one time is a slow process. The cast-iron melting pot hung from an eye-bolt set in the hanging wall, and a makeshift brick work was laid up around it to keep the heat from escaping. Once the blowtorch was lit and burning satisfactorily, we paid little attention to the zinc pot, except to add more zinc as the heat melted it down.

At times, pieces of ore too large for the crusher to handle came out of the mine, and they had to be broken up by blasting. This was done right in the crusher room by the crusher operators who kept a few sticks of dynamite on hand for the purpose.

The hooded melting pot, when it was not in use, made a dandy place to store dynamite, even though that was against mine safety rules and regulations. In times past we had found powder stashed away in the pot, so we always gave it a good going over before the furnace was fired up.

Somehow that morning we failed to find four sticks of dynamite that lay back inside the furnace hood. Apparently they had been tucked away out of sight by one of the operators for his own personal use. The idea the man had, perhaps, was that the other operators could darn well go to the powder magazine and get their own powder as they needed it. Or maybe he just forgot he'd put it there.

But when we smelled the sharp, pungent odor of burning dynamite, every man in the crusher room knew it was there. Instantly everything stopped, and all eyes turned to that roaring furnace. A thin pale blue smoke was just beginning to come from the furnace hood's door.

That was enough for us. The stampede was on, and it was a wild one.

At one end of the room a set of open zigzag stairs led to a mine level above. We went scrambling up the steps like a bunch of squirrels. When I reached the first landing I glanced back at the furnace, expecting it to blow and kill half of us. But I stopped and stared in amazement. What was happening was hard to believe.

Reese, the machinist from the mill shop and a close friend of mine, had pulled on a pair of asbestos welder's mitts, and was carefully lifting the burning sticks of dynamite from the furnace hood.

A small orange colored flame, sinister ashen, flickered from each one. Gently he laid stick after stick on the palm of his left hand, them carried them the full length of the crusher room and deliberately tossed the dynamite into the fine ore bins below.

He wound up his performance with a beautiful diving barrel-roll to get behind a pile of timbers for a little protection, should the powder explode when it hit on the bottom of the bins. None of us could figure out why it hadn't. Just our lucky day, I guess.

That evening Reese and I rode down from the mine in the same tram bucket, tired but relaxed and glad the day was over.

"Reese," I said, "What would you have done if the damned powder had exploded in your hand?"

"I'd have bent my jimmy-bar over that crusher operator's head."

"Oh, yeah, well, we know all crusher men go to heaven, because running a rock crusher is a hell of a job. But you better not go pounding on the Pearly Gates with a jimmy-bar. The Angel Gabriel might not let you in."

He's dumping a car in the 44 skip in the Shenandoah Mine in the 1930's. Zeke Zanoni Collection.

Inside the Shenandoah Mill around 1935. Zeke Zanoni Collection.

Accidents Are For Keeps

he ambulance wailed like a Banshee with a toothache as it came up behind me, and I had to pull off to the side to let it go racing by. It was easy to imagine the scene inside the gleaming vehicle—the accident victim secure on a stretcher wrapped in blankets to stave off the chill of shock, well-trained medics standing by with oxygen, plasma and a hypo if needed. These men and women with their equipment are angels of mercy in this accident prone, speed-crazed world. I knew a time when I would have given anything for a little of their attention and skill.

Back in the summer of 1926 I had a job as mill-hand at one of the large lead-zinc mines of Southwestern Colorado. A good job for a youngster just a year or two out of high school. One morning, shortly after going on shift, I was badly mauled in an accident at the company's mill. The memory of the long ordeal I endured has not faded through the years. A steel brace I wear strapped to my back never lets me forget.

It happened a little before noon while I worked the table floor (the lowest floor in the mill), taking samples and oiling the machinery—just routine duty. One of my chores was the care of a long, overhead line-shaft, driven by a large electric motor. The shaft in turn drove twelve "Wilfley Concentrating Tables", by means of wide, rubber transmission belts. The installation was a constant source of trouble and demanded so much work and attention that I hated the thing. But it had to be maintained.

Working along from table to table, I noticed a stench of burning oil, always a sure warning of trouble up on the line-shaft. Over near the motor drive end a journal was smoking hot. In order to get to it with my oil can and tools, I had to scramble up an old two-by-four ladder. Mill superintendents and shift bosses took a dim view of shutdowns for repairs because of burned-out equipment. So I tried to adjust and lubricate the journal and get it to cool off while the shaft was still running.

Perhaps it was carelessness on my part, or just plain disregard for the danger. But somehow in turning to climb down I snagged my overalls right across the small of my back, and they started to wind around the shaft. Lashed to the shaft by my own clothes I would be beaten to a pulp in seconds; it turned at 250 rpm. For me, the chips were down.

In the split-second before it dragged me from the ladder, I grabbed for something to try and pull myself free and managed to get hold of a water pipe with my left hand. Crazy with fear and pain, I fought that spinning bar of steel like a maniac, pitting my strength against the power of the motor in a grim tug of war. If I won I lived. If I lost I died. But manpower is no match for horsepower, and the strain almost tore my arm from the shoulder before it broke my grip on the pipe. Totally helpless I started to spin with the shaft's rotation. And I knew I'd never escape the whirling, smashing death just seconds away.

There happened to be enough space between the line-shaft and the cement wall so my head didn't strike as I made the first turns. My clothes began to rip away, and the thing peeled me out of them clean as a skinned rabbit. It hurled me against the cement wall with catapult force, and I fell to the floor twelve feet below. Even my socks were ripped off, although the white rubber mill shoes were still on my feet. I've never been able to understand how this could happen, but it did. Every stitch of clothing I'd worn formed a tight wad wrapped around the shaft.

Stunned and only partly conscious, I didn't realize I lay on the floor in the slime and muck, still alive. I couldn't move, get my breath or feel a thing. I didn't seem to have a body any more, just a head. And the thought came to me that possibly all but my head was a mangled mess wound up in the machinery. I wanted desperately to get up, just to prove I could stand on my feet. If I could do that, then my head and body were still attached. Finally I managed it and made a try for the stairs to the mill office on the floor above. But I staggered against a pulsating table deck. It struck me in the side and I went out cold.

A dim and bleary world greeted me when consciousness returned. The paralysis in my belly and chest had eased some. To be alive and lying there in the table spillage with a little air in my lungs was a wonderful relief. I crawled over to the steps and sat, trying to take stock of myself.

Then the pain came—so intense it made me sick. From my shoulders and back it seemed to flow in sheets to every part of my body. My left arm hung useless from the shoulder, and it had swollen so badly it scared me. My legs were not much better off either, but at least I could move them. Blood dripped from my nose, mouth and a dozen deep lacerations. I kept trying to get things in sharper focus not realizing both eyes were black and almost closed. A lot of skin had been burned away by my clothes when the shaft stripped me. Slowly I began to understand, I'd been seriously injured.

Calling for help was wasted effort—but I tried. No one could hear my voice above the crash and roar of the mill. An hour might pass before the shift boss came by on his rounds. I had only one out: climb the stairs to the office on the floor above for help.

I rested a few minutes and then faced the long flight of steps and started up. I panicked with the thought of falling back down again but kept telling myself, "Just a few more steps and you'll have it made." Those few steps took a lot of doing.

Finally when I staggered through the office door, the mill superintendent got the shock of his life. He all but fell over backwards out of his chair. "My God kid! What happened to you?" he yelled. Then he started firing questions without waiting for an answer. After he'd calmed down a little, I tried to tell him, but I don't think I made much sense. He phoned for a relief operator to come out and take my place. The operation of the mill was always uppermost in his mind.

Chris, my shift boss, came in about then, and I had to tell him what I thought had happened, all the while standing naked in the middle of the floor. He and the mill super just stood and gaped at me in astonishment. They couldn't think of a thing to do, and I was getting pretty light-headed. Chris came out of it first and rustled up a pair of old bib overalls and a jumper. "Here put'm on kid," he said. "You look like the wrong end of a butcher shop." I couldn't get into them so he helped me and then took some wet wiping waste and did what he could to clean up my face.

They thought it best I take the stage to town and have the doc at the company hospital look me over. Chris walked with me to the main office to make sure I got there. "You better wait here, Kelly will be along with the stage soon," he said. "And have the doctor take a good look at those cuts, as well as your arm." Chris figured he'd done all he could for me, and hurried back to the mill.

I didn't want to go into the office and sit down. I didn't want anyone to see me, so I waited outside and held onto the handrail to keep from falling. By the time Kelly pulled up in the old touring car he used for a stage, things were getting pretty vague. But that helped a lot as I eased myself onto the front seat. And I prayed I'd never have to move again.

Kelly was everyone's friend, as well as mine. "What happened to you?" he asked. "You fall off of the mountain or something?" I couldn't tell him much about the accident, and it miffed him a little. He took a long hard look at me but didn't say anything more and went about his business, delivering the stage freight to the mill. Then we drove over to the post office for the outgoing mail. A time consuming task. Kelly never pulled away from a stop without a complete run-down on the local gossip.

After the post office he headed for the company boarding house. "Come on in and have a cup of coffee, you look like you need it, and it's on the house," he said. "I'll have to see if the cook wants anything from town." I stayed in the car trembling uncontrollably from chills and shock. I wanted a cup of coffee like nothing else in the world right then. But the price I'd have to pay in pain to get it was too high.

When Kelly finally had all his details attended to, we went rattling down the canyon road to town. A long nine miles away. He did his best to miss the rocks and chuckholes, but I know he hit every one of them. Nauseated and weak, I chewed my lips, squinted my eyes and hung on. Shortly after we'd made a stop at a small hamlet to pick up the mail, Kelly redeemed himself. He gave me a drink of good bootleg whiskey from his bottle. It was a julep from heaven.

We made our last stop at a crossroad post office, and when Kelly came out with the mail sacks he said we had to make room for a lady passenger. He guessed I'd better get in the back seat. Somehow with his help I made the switch and climbed into the tonneau. It took a little time for the lights to stop flashing in my eyes and for me to quit swearing from the pain of moving about. Kelly hadn't mentioned the lady lived up a side road a mile or so.

Our passenger came out to the stage wearing her finery and a big smile. A trip to town on a bright summer day was no small event. Kelly, the gallant, grinned his welcome and held the door for her. She glanced up and saw me. Stifling a scream, she backed away from the car. I must have been a sight perched up on the freight and mail sacks, dressed in old dirty overalls, both eyes black and blood oozing from my nose and mouth. Trying to wipe it away only made it worse. If Kelly hadn't assured her I was harmless I think she would have run back to the house. Poor woman, I spoiled her trip. She sat on the very front edge of the seat, as close to the dash as she could, all the way to town.

Kelly brought the stage in late as usual. He'd run out of road, but not errands. First he saw the lady to her destination. Before he could open the door for her, she'd taken another look at me and fled. Naturally the post office was the next stop. It had priority and was the terminal for the stage line. "No need for you to walk over to the doctor," he said. "I have to drive by that way, and you may as well ride." A very friendly and considerate gesture on Kelly's part. He let me out in front of the hospital, and drove off.

From the sidewalk, I looked up at the second flight of stairs I'd faced that day. These were wide and not so high. But the steps seemed to be moving up and down in waves, and there was no handrail to hold onto. I wondered how in the world I'd climb up. I thought perhaps, if I spoke to them softly as a person would to a frightened or excited animal, they'd hold still. It worked, and I climbed up to the door and made my way inside.

Later one of the boys who was "Goldbricking" in the hospital, said a nurse found me standing in a hallway corner, chattering and shivering like a scared monkey. The pain in my body had been building in intensity all the time. I was far from rational, and I didn't want anyone near, for fear they might touch me.

I received the first pain killing shot three and a half hours after the accident. And when they'd finished with the necessary stitching and patching, I resembled a mummy more than a man. I couldn't walk or move without help. They'd strapped me to a plank, and I learned to know that piece of lagging very well indeed.

My score for the day was a broken back, a left arm all but yanked off my shoulder, some badly cracked ribs, and several joints that still give me some trouble. Sewing up the cuts, the bruises, and the skin I lost don't count. In time they built a steel frame to keep my back in line with my hips and shoulders, and I get along fine.

And friend, you there in the racing ambulance, too bad you were hurt. But since you were, you're in luck in that vehicle. There was a time equipment like that and trained personnel to man it didn't exist. For the unfortunate the going was rough. One thing hasn't changed much though. We still learn the hard way, that "accidents are for keeps."

Polly

Her name was Polly, graceful as a ballet dancer, nimble as a kitten, and her hair was a glossy light brown. Lovely soft black eyes belied the havoc she was capable of. She could move her seven hundred pounds of bone and muscle with speed and with astonishing results.

I'll have to admit, for a mule, she was beautiful.

Polly lived and worked down on B-Level in the old Sunnyside Mine and had been underground for quite some time. There is no opening to the surface on B-Level, and the mine hostlers had taken her down from Main Level on the cage at the Terry Shaft. This took a good deal of preparation and time, so once Polly was safely down on B, she had to live down there indefinitely. The company set up suitable living accommodations, and they were quite plush. She had a fresh bed of clean straw every day, the best feed obtainable, and her own toilet car.

She was young and strong, didn't shirk her work, knew the job thoroughly and would tolerate no foolishness at all. If her lamp went out, it had to be lit and adjusted. If there was something wrong with the train, she knew it instantly, and it was no go until the hostler corrected the trouble. She worked by command entirely, never driven or led, and wore her bridle as a miner wears his cap—to hold a lamp. The hostler rode the last car to do the braking, and when Polly started for the shaft with her train, there was no stopping until they pulled up at the station. It was a treat to watch her work with the "cager" putting a string of loaded cars through the diamond-switch and on to the cages to be hoisted to the ore bins above. Having disposed of the matter, and while the hostler was having a smoke, she'd step into her dining-room for a bite before they took the empties back for another load from the stopes.

A mine mule acquires some habits and a degree of sophistication not normal with the breed. Polly was the pet of B-Level and as spoiled and temperamental as a movie star. She loved ham sandwiches, apple pie, bananas, and a bottle of strawberry pop was her delight. But if some joker gave her an orange, she'd kick hell out of him or anyone within reach of her heels.

Animals become blind if they stay underground for long periods of time, without getting out to the sunlight each day. The state legislature passed a law requiring all animals working underground be stabled on the surface when off duty. So the company installed an electric mine locomotive on B-Level, and Polly lost her job.

Getting her back to the surface was nothing short of a miniature rodeo, with a mad mule for the star performer. She was too big to stand on the deck of a shaft cage; her head stuck out on one side and her rump on the other. So we had to fold her up to fit the available space. Four of us high school kids who were spending our summer vacation working on the mine bull-gang were sent down to B to help the hostlers.

Throwing and hog-tying a mule in the confines of an underground caging station is hectic. But somehow, the hostlers managed it. After her feet were tied up close to her body, we literally picked her up and set her on her rump on the cage deck, with her head up in the bonnet, and made her secure with ropes and safety bars. We had to work fast and get the ordeal over with before Polly gave up. Sometimes, animals give up and die when they become completely helpless, even though they've received no injury.

It wasn't in Polly's nature to give up. She fought us every step of the way, and when she couldn't move any more, she bawled and screamed. I've never heard such language from a mule in all my life. By using both cages, we all arrived on Main Level about the same time and laid Polly out on the station floor ready to turn her loose. All openings were blocked, and the cages set on the loading chairs to seal off the shaft, and we let her go. She chased the hoistman up the cable raise ladder and tried to climb up after him, and the rest of us scrambled for our lives. Polly was fighting mad, and someone was going to have to pay for the humiliating treatment she'd received. One of the boys ran to the boarding house and brought back an apple pie. She finally quieted down, decided to let by-gones be by-gones, and ate her pie.

We looked her over carefully to see if she'd been scratched or hurt in anyway. The hostlers and us kids were bruised and battered up, but that damned mule didn't have a mark on her. She'd lost her temper, and that was all.

Each day we let a little more daylight into the main level stable. It took about a month before her eyes were strong enough to stand the sunshine outdoors. For a while, she wore a dark veil to shade her eyes, and I think the hussy thought it was for her complexion.

I've often wondered what became of Polly after she lost her job. I hope her luck held out, and a ham sandwich and an apple pie came her way often enough.

This mule team is at Eureka, around 1900, loaded up with mine timbers. James Bell Collection, San Juan County Historical Society.

These are some of Louis Wyman Sr.'s horse teams, six up, moving ore from the Gold King Mine down Cement Creek just before 1900. Between 1895 and 1900 Wyman Sr. sold his entire outfit to the British government. The stock and equipment were trailed to New Orleans and shipped to South Africa for use in the Boer War. Grand Imperial Hotel Collection, San Juan County Historical Society.

The Big Horses

With the advent of aerial trams, the day of six-horse hitches, ore wagons and pack trains began to wane. Supplies went up to the mines and ore came down to the mills and railroads in ever-increasing volume. But mining companies still had to depend on a small, hard core of big horses and wagons to move the heavy pieces. Transformers, boilers, and compressors were too much for tram buckets, although a good deal of ingenuity is evident in the special carriers built to handle long or heavy loads over the cables.

Mine managers made it a point to have necessary repair parts that couldn't be shipped over trams moved up to the workings during the summer months. A "main shaft" for the primary crusher at the Sunnyside Mine was just such a piece. And should it break in the dead of winter the possibility of getting a new one up from Eureka was remote. Immediately after a breakdown and installation of the spare, another was made ready to be moved up when snow conditions permitted.

They used an ore wagon stripped down to the running gear (chassis) with a cradle made of strong timbers fitted to the bolsters to hold the shaft. It was never fastened or tied down to the cradle or wagon in any way. This was a necessary safety measure. In case of serious trouble on the trail, should the skinners lose control, the shaft could slide or roll free of the wagon and not drag horses and men to almost certain destruction in the depths of the canyon. There's a lot of weight in a bar of steel that large, and moving it up the mountain was a skinner's nightmare.

Usually a six-horse team was required, with one of the skinners riding and driving the leaders—cavalrystyle—and another handling the swing and wheel spans from a seat perched upon the load. The wagon was rigged so a fourth team could push from behind, and it was almost impossible to move the load uphill around a sharp turn without their help. If their luck was good, they'd make it half-way to the mine the first day. Then they would rough-lock all four wheels and let the wagon set until morning, while the teams went back to Eureka to be fed and stabled for the night. From half-way on up was by far the worst part of the trip, and if they arrived within three days, they counted themselves lucky.

Along in the 1920's, "caterpillar tractors" made their appearance in the San Juans. And the Sunnyside Mine—in need of a new crusher shaft—decided to try a tractor instead of teams for the big pull. At that time, caterpillars were not the diesel burning behemoths we have now. They were smaller gasoline machines, but still they were able.

In due course, a wagon was rigged with a short trailer tongue and the tractor coupled on. Eureka turned out to a man to see the show and place a few side bets. The outfit pulled out on time and moved up-grade north of the mill, yanked its load around a hairpin turn that gave the skinners and their teams so much trouble, and headed for the mine. Word came down before noon that it had arrived safely, and was on its way back to Eureka with an empty wagon.

And then another fabulous machine, the Coleman truck, put in an appearance and its performance was equally spectacular. Only machines could satisfy the ever-increasing demands for more and more of everything, and the days of teams, wagons, and pack trains had passed.

But, by any measure, the big horses were magnificent. They and their wagons faded into limbo with the Sunnyside and the old town of Eureka. It seemed as though they went into their stables at the day's end, and never came out again.

This is the Washington Vertical Hoist in the Sunnyside Mine, around 1929. James Hook Collection, San Juan County Historical Society.

Tommyknocker Hoistman

Each time a man quits the sunlight to grub around underground in a mine, he enters another world.

Perhaps it isn't a part of purgatory, but I think the devil would feel quite at home down there. As the last feeble glimmer of daylight at the portal flickers out, a realm of utter blackness closes in. Damp cold fills every small tunnel and opening. The warm safety of sunshine and daylight is gone. A man will do well to accept the ways of the spirit denizens who (according to some folks) live down there.

I'm not overly superstitious. I pay little attention to ghost stories, nor do I get hung up over "taboos". However, in some ways thirteen doesn't appeal to me, though I'll bet on number thirteen on a roulette wheel any time. But never number twenty-three. I have a silly habit of knocking on wood or the side of my head when a cat crosses in front of me. It's one of those hangovers from childhood ghost stories that made me afraid to go to bed in the dark. So now I don't have much patience with people who think there are spirits running around loose, or say there is some truth in old wives' tales.

But having to work underground from time to time, I was bound to make the acquaintance of a "Leprechaun, Elf, or Tommyknocker," the secretary for the "Spook Union" sent out to work as my helper. Learning the little fellow's name was a problem too. I used a different one each time I spoke to him until I found one he seemed to like. In my case, every time I addressed him as "Morris", (that was before the tomcat of TV fame) things moved along just fine. If I neglected the formality, first one thing after another went haywire until I remembered about him, apologized, and asked his forgiveness. The little punk could be a lot of help if he was happy and willing to cooperate.

I had a real run-in with Morris one time in the old Shenandoah Mine. The company had started development on the three hundred level, and I'd been sent up there late one afternoon on an emergency repair job. The upper levels were served by a small skip which slid up and down the raise on a wooden slide. A man could ride the thing if he wished, but climbing the manway ladder was a lot safer. However, I tossed my tool sack onto the skip deck then gave old Dave the hoistman a signal to take me up to three hundred. I'd asked him to let the skip hang up there at the station, if I didn't call for it before he went off shift. That way I could lower my tools and broken parts myself, after I'd climbed down the raise to the main level hoist room.

"C'mon, Morris," I said. "Get on, let's go. I don't want to hang out here half the night."

A short time after tally I finished the job and went back to the station. Old Dave had left the skip hanging there as he said he would. On the off chance that he might have waited a little while after shift to give me a ride down, I stepped on and signaled the hoistroom "Man on, lower away".

To my surprise, the slip started down the slide quite slowly, as it should when transporting men and material. For once I was in luck. I should have known better—hoistmen never wait a minute past tally to help a repairman up out of the hole or down from the level above. I began to wonder why it happened I was getting a ride down after shift had gone off. Somebody was down there running the hoist for me, that was for sure.

By the time the skip was halfway down it had picked up too much speed. It was rattling down the slide too fast for safety. Old Dave seemed in an awful hurry to get me down from three hundred. He never slowed up. The skip hit the main level station with a good solid thump. My legs folded up—I went sprawling out onto the track in front of the hoistroom.

When I'd decided there were no broken bones between my head and heels, I scrambled to my feet, heading for the hoistroom door with just one thing in mind— knock some sense into a cantankerous old lever-man's head.

But there was nobody on the hoist that I could see, nor had there been since tally. Then I began to understand just what had happened. Morris had been running the hoist in Dave's place. Morris was mad at me because I'd forgotten to ask him to ride down on the slip. He'd whisked down the manway and set the hoist handbrake to give the skip a good hard landing when it hit the main level station. I knew he was perched up on the hoistman's chair grinning at me, so I threw a piece of rock at him. All I hit was a clock on a shelf above the hoist—smashing it to bits.

"Listen, Morris," I said, "That's enough foolishness for one day. You darned near killed me with that ride on the skip. And now I have to buy a new clock. Call it off. I'm sorry I didn't invite you to ride down with me. And now I have to buy a new clock for Dave. But you knew there was no hoistman down here and tricked me into thinking there was. Now cut out the clowning and let's be friends. I'll admit you can run that hoist as well as anyone. So why don't you do the job right once in a while? Come on, walk out to the surface with me, I'm tired and want to get down off the hill."

If I could get the little devil out to daylight, I'd hang one on him that would even the score for the day. I had made up my mind to give Morris the cussing of his life. Down the drift, daylight had just come into view at the portal, when the bottom of my tool sack split wide open. Everything fell into the drainage ditch beside the track. I had to get down on my hands and knees while I fished around in a foot and a half of muddy water to find them. The little imp could read my mind, so he'd taken one last poke at me before I could get out of his reach.

Like I said, I'm not overly superstitious, but underground where the sun never shines is another world. They have their own rules down there. Every time I got out of line Morris straightened me out in a hurry. For the most part the little pest and I made out fairly well. Several times he saved me from a serious accident with a warning any dumb bloke would understand.

You'll Have to Tell Old Jim

Billy and Jack didn't choose their home. A horse and burro don't have that privilege. But Jim exercised his rights and chose a snug cabin in the Colorado Rockies. He said he'd traded The Old Santa Fe Trail, The Texas Panhandle, and a few Longhorns when he made the deal. Anyway, that's where I, as a young man with rambling feet, made friends with the old mountaineer, his horse, and packburro. A friendship that ran down through the years in easy stride, asking little and giving much.

For the few who live there, "The Rockies" can be a land of hardship and high adventure or indolent and easy, depending on one's luck. The winters are cruel and frozen in their white splendor, and the summer sunshine is warm and benign. Ghost towns and abandoned miners' camps populate the valleys and parks. And like dreams born of great hope and courage that came to nothing, they slowly vanish. If you'll look down in the southwest corner of your map of Colorado, you will find "The San Juans" marked in heavy type. Just a little bit of the world, some say, but what a vast paradox it is. Sometimes small, unimportant things, like an old gray horse and burro, become so vital they change the course of a man's life.

That's the way it was with Billy and Jack. About sundown they usually made it up to the barn for a handout of grain. They also received a good cussing, delivered in the soft drawl of the old mountaineer. He seemed to think a burro should be cussed "regular," as he put it. "It's the only thing they understand," he said. I could never see that it had much effect on them, one way or the other. Jim enjoyed it, and I marveled at the multitude of sins the two animals were guilty of. One thing was sure, they were a pampered pair of characters.

On Saturdays, from early spring until the snow closed the trails to all but men on snowshoes, Billy and Jack made a trip to town, seven miles down the canyon and seven miles back. They did it in utter boredom. I don't think I ever saw two animals so completely indifferent. Jim's need of supplies and his mail were a nuisance they grudgingly tolerated. Billy would amble along the trail with Jim up in the battered McClellan saddle, sitting as straight as a cavalry captain. Behind the cantle the ever-present yellow slicker was tied in the smallest possible roll, with a canteen just below on the off side. A tall, stiff-brimmed hat, black as a new piece of coal, sat level and true above the gray eyes and sweeping Texas mustache. Always he wore a suit coat over a clean shirt and tie and his brown corduroys tucked into high-laced miner's boots. Of course, Billy had been brushed a bit too. It was more a habit on Jim's part; there was little hope of improving the old gray much.

Burros can't be improved either. You just have to endure them; they're changeless in habit and nature. Once the pack-saddle cinch was tightened, Jack became a strict conformist to all his donkey characteristics. He would not lead, nor could he be driven. But wherever Billy went he followed right behind, step for step, turn for turn and stop for stop. Whatever the attachment was, it was stronger than picket rope or bridle rein. He was a big burro, almost as large as the horse. Sometime in his past the cartilage of his left ear had been broken. He had no control over the ear at all. It flopped forward and out at a silly angle, while the right one performed naturally. The good side of his head seemed to reveal jackass sense, but the other was a hardpan blank. At times, just looking at the ludicrous old fellow would send Jim off on a long run of profanity so highly descriptive even Jack paid attention. I think the old devil knew he and the horse had things completely reversed—work one day and rest six.

Many a time I stopped by to sit with Jim over a good cup of coffee, laced just right with "Mountain Dew." And they would pay the cabin a social call, standing with their heads through the doorway begging for a little sugar or left-over hotcake. Life in the valley was slow and easy, and the time slipped by almost unnoticed.

Then one day Jim walked the four miles up the canyon to my camp to tell me the animals had disappeared completely.

Billy and Jack hard at work or should I say headed to the cabin in hopes of a handout. Louis Wyman Collection.

It's not unusual for idle stock to wander and with a little wrangling they are found and brought home. All is then forgiven until it happens again. I let Jim have my trail horse to use while he looked for Jack and Billy. Nig, as I called him, was an original and, like some people, born to raise Cain. I was about half glad to get rid of him for a time. The question was—could he and Jim come to terms? By the end of a week the horse had settled to his work, and they were getting along fairly well. Strays ordinarily show up in a day or so, but time passed, and he could find no sign of them. I didn't know it then, but Jim and I were launched on a quest that endured until the snow drove us down to our dooryards.

I took to riding the timberline country, hoping to find some trace of the lost stock. August slipped by. September came with a little brown showing here and there in the mountain alders. Time was getting short. The autumn gold went flooding through the aspens, and the sumac turned blood red. Somehow the spruce seemed to grow even darker against the blaze of color. Through the days I listened to the cold dry wind chattering incessantly to the tall bunch grass. And the tiny creeks lay quiet and still in their pools, too chilled and spent to stir.

Sometimes I would catch a glimpse of a black horse and his rider on a distant ridge or slope or the marks of Nig's steel shoes in the trail told me they had passed that way. Often we met as we rode in at nightfall, and I became concerned about Jim. Fatigue was stamped on the old man's face. It was bone-deep exhaustion and disappointment. I felt, and I think he did too, that we would never find them. But he wouldn't give up and I could do no less. The black horse and the old man were a remarkable pair. One was dead tired and the other at the very peak of perfection. Nig carried his rider with that tough arrogance only the proud can muster. Under Jim's hand the black had become a man's horse, schooled and trained, with a spirit as wild as the mountain wind.

Winter came early that year. The snow pushed its way, storm by storm, down from the high peaks and basins into the parks and meadows that had long since turned brown and lifeless. The world became a white waste where nothing moved, except a black horse and his rider. Jim was broken and exhausted. I hadn't fully realized how much the loss of Billy and Jack meant to him. They were his companions, and the three of them were almost a family. Sure, there were other horses and burros to be had, but Billy and Jack were individuals and a way of life. All the weeks of riding brought no clue, and the long trail was finished; further effort was useless. I wished Jim's distress was buried under the deep snow with our failure.

I remember I was sweating out the trip back to camp after a two week Christmas holiday in town, and pushing hard, with a storm riding my back trail. It eases the strain and loneliness of a long day to live in retrospect while the slow miles shuffle by under your snowshoes. For a mountain man to lose his stock is an unforgivable fault. I recalled as much of those last weeks as I could. Nowhere could I find an answer, but I knew there must be one.

The quest was dead, and Jim had given up, so I shook my mind free of the puzzle. Camp was at hand and a welcome sight. It was snug and deep in the snow. Best of all it marked the trail's end and that longed-for moment when I could ease the heavy pack from my shoulders at the cabin door and stand the rifle against the wall. All day it had pulled at my arms like a shrinking thong. The freedom of movement without snowshoes and harness is pure joy and for a time your feet seem to be weightless. Trail's end brings a warmth and a chance to relax and rest.

From the stoop most of the clearing was visible. While I rested a bit, I idly searched the snow for a telltale sign, some indication of the trivial things that happen about a camp while you're away. And sure enough, over at the eastern end of the park, where an abandoned miner's shack stood, the snow was trampled and marred by many feet. There appeared to be a well-trodden track running back into the timber, and I thought I glimpsed a shadowy movement just at the tree line. Again I bent to the snowshoe harness. I would have to find out who my neighbors were. The warmth and rest I wanted so badly must wait.

All around the old building I found the tracks of a small pack of coyotes. They had been going in and out of the shack through a small hole low in a side wall. This in itself was strange. Coyotes rarely venture close to human habitation. As I moved up, I fingered the safety on my rifle. A lucky shot might bring a prime ten dollar pelt, which was no small day's wages. Then again I might even get a second shot. But my visions of a few easy "bucks" faded like the trail the coyotes left. Nothing moved, so I went over to a window opening for a look inside.

Brutal and cruel mischance had laid the scene. On the floor were the wasted carcasses of Billy and Jack. I had found them! Seldom does a trail end in such calamity. Their paunches were ripped open and the coyotes had been working from the inside out, as scavengers do. In dismay and wild anger I slammed open the door and went in. Standing there in the fading light, my mind reeled with the intensity of the horror that lay strewn about the floor. The "Imps of Hell" had out-done themselves on this one, and now they played their gruesome drama back for me, scene by slow scene. How they must have capered with glee as Jim and I ranged over mountain and valley in our search. And they held court in that one small room.

The story came full toned and clear out of the past. It told how Billy and Jack were grazing in the clearing on a warm August afternoon and, as usual, the stock flies were a bit bothersome. And it was their habit to take refuge in whatever shade was close by. The boxcar-roofed shack was made to order, so they tramped through the open door to the welcome coolness inside and oblivion.

I don't know if it was the Imps, the wind, or if one of the animals bumped the door shut to seal them in their crypt forever. How many long days and nights did they stand and wait for Jim to come and get them? Time and again they must have seen him ride by on the far side of the valley, in the early morning or late evening, and they waited. Perhaps Billy nickered softly for help from time to time, yet no one heard. Just a step or two from the door the creek bounced by on its rocky bed and not a drop could they reach. Harebells and lush mountain clover grew thick about the walls, and they stood helpless; the door had closed. Slowly their old heads drooped lower in their agony, while the Imps applied the screws of thirst and starvation.

Billy had gone down first. He lay with his head to the window opening, where for so long he had begged and called to us to come. The tough old burro had stood his dying watches alone, until thirst and hunger cut him down, and he lay with his head on the front legs of the horse.

Men who live close to nature and much of the time alone, become accustomed to natural death among animals. So it was not the partly consumed carcasses strewn about the floor that nauseated me, but the shocking tragedy that was enacted here that was as stunning as physical pain. I was sick that such a thing could happen within rifle shot of camp.

I tore what boards I could from the walls and smashed the crude packing case furniture into kindling. In each of the four corners of the room I lighted fires and fanned them into high flames before I stumbled coughing and choking out the door into the cold winter dusk.

There are a few hours of grace before a winter storm breaks over the Rockies. You watch the gathering forces as the zenith fades into a gray pall of snow cloud and wind-blown scud. The peaks and ridges become blurred in the diffused and shadowless light and you sense the power of the coming storm in the muted world about you. The night comes quickly with the first swirling gusts. I looked back across the white clearing. A pillar of fire rose clear and bright against the darkness and coming storm.

Was it the wild screech of the wind as it gained the clearing? Or was it just my imagination? But it seemed to come from somewhere out of the night. "You'll have to tell old Jim." Maybe it was just the coyote pack, back there in the timber, crying their protest.

Now, early in the year, the snow could be plowed. Here, Louis Wyman Sr. drives one of the town's teams. Helen Fleming Collection, San Juan County Historical Society.

Blockade

Silverton is the dead-end terminal for a short but long-lived narrow gauge railroad. The tracks traverse fifty miles of the upper canyon of the "Rio de las Animas Perdidas," one of the most rugged in the entire San Juan Mountains. If there is a purgatory between the boundaries of heaven and hell, it could well be the Animas Canyon in the winter time. Only the fabulous wealth of the mines could have influenced men to attempt to lay rails through the treacherous defile. In those early years, Silverton depended upon the steam trains year around, to move ore out to market and bring supplies in.

Usually by October, everyone was fortified with provisions to last well into the spring months. But the winter of 1926-27 was a record one for deep snow and avalanches. All roads and highways had been abandoned to King Winter, and the town dug in for a long siege—completely isolated except for the telephone and telegraph. Occasionally, a hardy adventurer would brave the white void of snow and cold, fighting his way through the canyon to bring word of the railroad's progress in reaching the snowbound mining town. Often the gains of a week were lost to a howling blizzard that turned the canyon into a death trap, and the crews had to be pulled out until avalanche danger lessened.

By late March, the community had been sixty days without a train. Although coal and supplies were ample, feed for the dairy stock was critically short. Outgoing mail had piled up in the post office, and the doctor was running out of pills. Now and then, some young men would take advantage of a good day and pull a toboggan load of first class mail down to the trains, bringing back what incoming mail they could. But this didn't solve the problem by any means. So Mayor Baker and the town council had persuaded the postal service to advertise for bids on a contract to transfer the United States Mail to and from Silverton by whatever means possible. The contract was to run until the snow blockade lifted.

Only one bid of fifty cents a pound was received, submitted by the Shawn Bros. Freighting Co. The contract was duly awarded to them. But a precedent was set by the contract price, and fifty cents a pound became the standard freight rate for anything transferred from the train into town, regardless of who did the transferring.

Train crews fought stubbornly to gain a mile or two a day against the almost impenetrable barrier of ice and snow they faced; they were still fifteen miles down the canyon from town when Shawn and his packers went to work on their contract. They brought thirty head of pack mules from winter pasture for the job. Before the month of March was half gone, they were hot-footing it over the snowslides and drifts on a trail tramped hard as cement. They worked in two strings, one coming and one going, passing each other about half way on the trail. Meeting the pack train at the post office in the evening became the big event of the day.

But then the snow would mount. The businesses would keep their places open, but skis, snowshoes, and sleighs became the way to get around in the early 1900's. Besides, who needed roads. The train always came in.

Looking up and down Greene Street,

which is hardly green. Ray Doud Photos, Jim Bell/Gerald Glanville Collection.

His Honor Mayor Baker called a special meeting of the town council to brief them on a trip he'd made down country, riding one of Shawn's pack mules over the transfer trail both ways. As usual, he sat in his chair at the head of the council table. Mayor Baker was a big man—not fat, just big. A typical small-town politico. He worked hard at the job of town mayor, and people liked him and trusted him.

"Gentlemen," he said, "for some time, I've thought we might use the mail contract to move feed into town by parcel post. It looked like the only chance to save the kids' milk supply as well as the dairy stock. The problem was: How? I didn't want to say too much about it until I was sure, because of the disappointment if a plan couldn't be worked out."

The mayor stood up and rubbed the backs of his legs.

"Hope the devil has to ride a pack mule for the rest of his life," he muttered and reluctantly eased himself down on the chair again. "Man, am I sore."

Well, all right, sometimes it just got too bad, and the train didn't always come in. And that's when the trouble began. Here a work train moves the D&RGW ditcher ox into a snowslide area during the 1926-27 blockade. Louis Wyman Collection, San Juan County Historical Society.

He took a deep breath and continued.

"Of course, the town clerk got into the ruckus with me right off. She's been handling the paper work and telephone calls for some time now. And she battled it out by herself when I was out of town. The council and town owe her a big vote of thanks."

"Let the minutes of this special meeting so state," Ralph, one of the more valuable council members, said. The clerk bowed prettily and smiled her thanks.

"Well," the mayor continued, "we got in touch with the postal department and explained the situation and what we had in mind to do about it. They told us that if baled hay conformed in size and weight to postal regulations, it could be shipped parcel post to any place in the United States served by the department."

"Where in the world can anyone find hay baled like that?" Ralph wanted to know. "And who's going to pay the postage on it."

Several other members of the council voiced concern about the possible expense the town might incur. While the postal department paid the contract bill, they certainly didn't intend to pay the postage, too.

"When I got down to the lower country," the mayor went on, "I looked up a rancher I know quite well. He said he had plenty of hay in the stack and could bale it in fifty-pound bales. And he did.

"Next, I called our senator and representative in Denver. I explained what we intended to do, and that the postage bill could be considerable. They said to push ahead, that there was emergency money available. This thing has caught the public's interest statewide. Right now, we are front page news. When I got back home last evening, Lena called and said she had a telegram from Denver. Lena, will you read it, please?"

"Yes, sir."

State Capitol
Denver, Colorado
March 20, 1927

The Honorable Mayor Baker
And City Council
Silverton, Colorado

  Dear Arthur:

  Senator Jones and Representative Stillman have just informed me on the situation in Silverton, and the action you and the council have taken. I wish to extend my congratulations on your resourcefulness in this time of emergency.

  We have set in motion the machinery that should relieve your town of any abnormal financial problems relating to the snow blockade. Keep us well informed on conditions there. Again, my congratulations on a job well done.

Alva B. Adams
Governor, State of Colorado

"Thank you, Lena. Let the minutes of the meeting show the telegram was read while the council was in session. Now you fellas know as much as I do. We can work out the details at a regular meeting. I'd like to hear a motion to adjourn. It's getting late."

But before a motion could be passed, Ernie Shawn pushed the council room door open and came in, his spur rowels chiming faintly with each step. He nodded a silent greeting to the mayor and the council members, and without hesitation, moved a chair back from the table and sat down. He pulled off his gloves, carefully laid his hat on the table beside him, and took off the black skullcap that covered his ears. With aggravating slowness, he rolled a brown paper cigarette and stretched out his legs to ease the cramp of a long day in the saddle.

Mayor Baker's smile broadened to a grin of amusement as he watched the silent mule skinner and the fidgeting councilmen. The man is solid leather, he thought —leather chaps, leather boots, leather coat, and leather rosette buttons. His face is the color of leather, too. I'll bet he's so tough, he don't even feel the saddle when he mounts up. And he's going to bust this council meeting wide open if he don't say something pretty soon.

"Ernie," the mayor said finally, "we're glad you dropped in. What's the news from the canyon?"

"Not much, Art. But I'll tell you men this. There's never been so much snow and ice in that canyon before. This will be the longest blockade we've ever had."

"Are you unloading the mail over at the post office now?" a councilman asked.

"No, Ralph, I rode on ahead. I wanted to see if there was any change in your plans. The packs are heavy today, and I don't want the mules standing under their loads longer than I have to. Pedro will be pulling in with the string and the mail in a little while."

"Ernie, I don't think there's any ..."

Mayor Baker's voice faded out as Silverton's dairyman stormed into the afternoon meeting, blasting their complacency out the window. His blue eyes burned with frustration and anger as he slammed a rifle down on the table. The tension he created held the council expectant and silent. Every eye in the room was fastened on the squat, heavy figure. His baleful stare never left the mayor's face.

"What in damnation is the matter with you, Carl?" Mayor Baker's voice had a frosty edge to it as he spoke. "There's not a man in this room who is not your friend. Why did you come bursting in here and slam a high-power rifle down on the table in front of us, and never say a word? Damn it, man, speak!"

"I'll tell you what's wrong in short order, Mr. Mayor. Weeks ago, I told you that if the blockade lasted much longer, I'd be out of feed for my cows. Well, gentlemen, time has run out. And as far as I can see you've done nothing but sit around on your butts. The freight rate of fifty cents a pound makes a bale of hay that's worth only a buck and a half in the field cost me over fifty dollars at my barns. No dairyman can feed hay at that price."

Carl's voice broke with emotion, but the tension in the council chamber had eased a bit. The clerk's fingers worked their magic with pencil and notebook, and she glanced up, waiting for Carl to continue.

"Listen, men," he went on, "I tried to get Ernie and his skinners to trail the herd out to the railroad work train so I could ship 'em down country to where there's feed. They said they couldn't get five miles with 'em on that narrow trail. Taking care of dairy cows on a drive down through the canyon in subzero weather is impossible. Ernie says they'd die of exposure before he could get 'em half way through, and I know he's right." Carl was no weakling. It bothered the mayor to see him begging for help. There was no longer any hostility in His Honor's manner as he watched the broken man across the table from him.

And, at first, attempts would be made to walk the long miles down the avalanche covered rails and haul the mail back to town on toboggans. Here Louis Wyman and Kid Taylor take a break, 1927. Louis Wyman Collection, San Juan County Historical Society.

"I can't let my stock stand in the barns and slowly starve to death," Carl went on. "I have to have feed now. In another three days, there won't be a single quart of fresh milk in town for the kids. And I won't have a dairy."

He struggled a moment for control.

"There's my gun on the table. Day after tomorrow, I'll start butchering, and it sure as hell ain't going to be a very pleasant time at the Silverton Dairy. Any of you fellows want to come out and help with the killing?"

The mayor tapped on the table for attention.

"Carl," he said, "this meeting was called so I could brief the council on what I was able to do about your feed problem, so the kids wouldn't lose their milk supply. But you come bounding in here with blood in your eye, and acting like a fool. We've got news for you. Sit down, man. Sit down!"

The dairyman raised his clenched fist and took a deep breath to roar his reply back at the mayor. But before he could speak, the council room door burst open and old Coop—Silverton's postmaster—stormed in, doing a good job of roaring on his own. He'd been so intent on getting across the street to the Town Hall that he was still in his sleeve-protectors, blue denim apron and eye shield. Coming in out of the evening cold had fogged up his glasses, so he could hardly see. But he located Carl standing with his hand in the air, too surprised to remember he was about to shake his fist at Mayor Baker.

"They told me you were here, milk peddler!" he yelled. "Do you know there's a whole string of pack mules standing right there in front of the post office? And every damn one is loaded with hay instead of mail? Silly little half bales, stamped and shipped with the postage paid, all for that stinking dairy of yours. But you're not going to make a cow barn out of my post office. I won't let Ernie unload that hay in the building. I'm gonna dump it in the street. To hell with it, and you too."

Coop's long frame all but doubled up on the floor as Carl brushed him aside in a headlong rush for the door. He ran out to the plowed walk in front of the Town Hall, and stopped dead still. There they were, fifteen big mules, each one loaded with two small half-bales of hay. Their loads added up to fifteen hundred pounds of good rich alfalfa hay.

Carl scrambled over the snow banks to get to the first mule and almost fearfully read the shipping tag attached to one of the half-bales. Neatly typed on a weather-proof tag together with the proper number of canceled stamps was his name, and Silverton Dairy, Silverton, Colorado.

For a minute or two, he rested his forehead against the mule's warm neck. One hand gripped the close-cropped mane, and the other fussed blindly with the basket-hitch that lashed the bale to the packsaddle. When he straightened up, a hayseed or two had somehow gotten into his eyes, but the sag had disappeared from his broad shoulders.

Coop met him on the sidewalk in front of the post office. The cantankerous old man wished Carl a pleasant trip to hell, and would he please take his damn hay with him?

Carl thanked the old fellow and gave him a clap on the back that all but knocked him out from behind his glasses.

But as time dragged on and the slides kept coming, supplies became desperately low and pack strings were put to work making the long haul back up the canyon to town.

Unloading in front of the Post Office. Photos by Ray Doud, Jim Bell/Gerald Glanville Collection.

Baled hay arriving via parcel post created some excitement for everyone but Ernie Shawn. The string of mules standing in the street represented a long, hard day's work to him, and he was in no hurry to leave the comfortable chair at the council table. The entire council had grabbed their coats and snow boots, and quit the chambers in a group. The mayor and Lena had their pictures taken while she held the bridle reins of the lead horse. But the cold drove the clerk and the mayor back to the Town Hall office, where they could watch the action from a window. Lena began to sniffle and wipe her nose.

Ernie spoke up from the chair where he'd just finished his cigarette.

"You catching a cold, Miss Lena?" he asked.

"No, sir, Mister Shawn. I just can't help crying a little, I'm so happy. The hay on those mules is just beautiful. It's been terrible wondering what was to become of those poor dairy cows if the mayor's plan to get feed for them didn't work out. Now they can all be saved, and the children will have their milk, too. This has been one of our nicest days."

"What do you want to do about old Coop over at the post office, Arthur? He made more noise than a Rocky Mountain canary."

"He'll be all right," the mayor replied. "He's just sore he didn't get to read the postal card first. When you get the sacked mail off, why not pull over to Carl's barns with the hay? I think he'll meet you with a team and sled after this. Better get old Coop to release the hay to you or Carl first."

"Yeah, I can do that. Be easier than holding that old goat down while we pile the hay in on top of him. Well, I'll go help Pedro finish up and get the stock stabled. It's going to be damn cold tonight."

"If you see any of the councilmen over at the post office, Ernie, tell 'em to get back over here," the mayor said. "We've got a meeting that hasn't been properly adjourned."

"I'll give 'em the word. See you next trip."

"Say, Ernie, don't you and that bandito Pedro give our good postmaster a bad time, now."

The stockman pulled his skullcap down over his ears and stood up. There was a little gleam of humor in his brown eyes as he picked up his hat and gloves.

"No, no," he said. "I'm tired, and Pedro is soft-hearted. But that 30-30 there on the table; I was wondering if you're going to use it for a gavel. It's real convincing, Arthur."

The mayor's face flushed a bit, but before he could put a fitting reply together, Ernie's spur rowels were tinkling in the outer office.

"That damn mule skinner and his mules," he muttered as he shifted his weight in the chair. "Anybody dumb enough to associate with 'em ought to have a sore behind." Within the hour, Mayor Baker had a quorum seated at the council table and brought the meeting back to order.

"Gentlemen," he said, "we've had an interruption or two this evening, but now we may be able to adjourn the meeting. There's nothing that can't wait for a regular session. Somebody move we adjourn."

"Not yet," Carl said as he came in, stamping snow from his boots. His face was red from the outside cold and smiling with good humor.

"You again," groaned several of the council members.

"Yeah, it's me again," and his smile broadened to a wide grin. With a flourish and a bow, he presented the clerk with a large bag of peppermint candy.

Then, he turned to the council table and opened a box of good cigars and passed them around.

"Now," he said. "Go ahead and adjourn."

As he went out the door, someone yelled to come back and get his old shootin' iron.

"Hell, man, I got no time for that now," he called back.

Everyone had cleared out and gone home. The mayor sat alone in the evening quiet, tired and wishing he were home, too. He thought he heard a light step behind him. Before he could turn, soft lips kissed his cheek and were gone.

"Fool girl," he said. "I wonder how the good Lord happened to be so careless and put nice young people and mules in the same world?"

When he stepped out on the street, he met fifteen of them. Free of their packs, they paced along behind the lead horse, ears forward and heads up. They knew the day's work was over. The stable was next, with feed and rest.

Ernie touched his hat brim, and Mayor Baker caught the flash of white teeth in Pedro's smile as they rode by. Then he turned and walked on toward home.

"Guess we can't get along without the damn things," he said aloud.

But he listened for the last creak of leather and the tinkle of the tall mule's bell.

And finally, in a joyous moment after months of effort, the train would push through the canyon to arrive in the beleagered town. Grand Imperial Hotel Collection, San Juan County Historical Society.

We Lost the Shovel

ostalgia is a jewel case where treasured memories are kept. Some glow softly with the sheen of pearls. Some sparkle and flash, recalling the excitement that lifts the spirit once again. And the others, like "Apache Tears", are darkly beautiful.

That spring, as usual, the railroad was having trouble with wet snow slides. The weather had turned warm enough to cause them to start running. They were piling up in the canyon, blocking the tracks for days at a time. Spring snow is so wet and heavy that shoveling it by hand seems to be the only way it can be moved. Locomotives equipped with snowplows are all but helpless trying to plow through the slides.

At times, we no sooner had a section of track cleaned up than the slush would come tumbling down off the cliffs, and we'd have to run for safety. A man who didn't have a healthy respect for those avalanches could get hurt. When the "all clear" signal came, we'd go back and start in digging again. All the work that had been done was wiped out by the slide. Heaving snow out of a deep cut for eight or ten hours is back-breaking labor. It helped a little to cuss the slides, the railroad or your shovel. A man just had to vent his feelings on something.

A mile or so down the track from the old snowshed, one slide in particular always gave the railroad a lot of trouble each spring. Robert Salfisberg and I were working in the cut which was about twelve feet deep at that point. We were shoveling snow up to men who stood on a shelf half-way up on the side, and they in turn threw it up over the top.

Robert and I were not buddies, but always the best of friends. Many times we found ourselves involved in the same action and would team up for the job, the trip or whatever. He was a whirlwind of a man, with terrific strength, speed, and perfect muscle coordination. To him, life was just one big hilarious romp. He seemed to be laughing all the time. Fear was something he didn't know anything about. I've seen him walking on his hands around the balustrade on the second floor of the Silverton Town Hall rotunda—just because some fool was willing to bet he couldn't. To compete and win was the very essence of life to Robert. He was a good man to be with on the trail or on the job.

We were working down on the bottom of the cut and, as usual, giving each other a good-natured ribbing about one thing or another. Now and then, one of us would try to knock a top-man off his shelf with a shovelful of snow, just to relieve the drudgery with a little fun. The warning cry of "Slide! Slide!" sounded up and down the line of shovelers. It was time to go. The work and fun turned into a wild scramble for safety.

Robert and I ran for the end of the trench where a set of steps had been cut in the bank. He got there first and went up and out like a scared mountain goat. I almost made it, too. My head was just even with the top of the snowbank when the slip—a small snow slide—hit me. The snow filled the trench level full and pinned me against the side with just a little of my face and head sticking out. It was like being buried in cement. I don't think I have ever felt so abandoned and helpless in my life. The slide had knocked the wind out of me and packed the snow in so tight that I could hardly expand my lungs enough to breathe. Yelling for help was impossible. A man has to have air in his lungs to do that. All I could do was stare at Robert and the crew running across a snow-bridge over the river.

He must have suddenly realized I wasn't with him. I saw him stop and look around. After a moment, he saw my head sticking out of the slide and came leaping back, waving his shovel in the air like a wild man. He started to dig at the hard packed snow around me as if he were possessed. In half a minute or less, he had me uncovered down to my knees.

Then he stopped digging and handed the shovel to me.

"Here," he said. "If you're too lazy to run, why should I dig you out." He squatted down on his heels laughing at my predicament, and offering some very pointed comments while he watched me struggle to get free.

I was still working to get my feet loose when the cry "Slide! Slide!" echoed through the canyon again. I couldn't run; my feet were still held fast in the hard-packed snow. The men across the canyon were yelling, "Run for it, you damn fools! The slide is coming right down on top of you!"

"Give me that shovel," Robert hissed and wrenched it out of my hands. With a tremendous effort he literally lifted me out of my hole on his shovel blade along with the broken snow. It was not in his nature to run and save himself, leaving his "pardner" there to be struck down in a slide. We went together, or we didn't go at all. He had given me a chance to live, and we ran for our lives—clearing the avalanche track a split second before the slide struck.

It was a big one, carrying with it rocks, dead timber, and chunks of ice big as barrels from the mountainside above. The place where I'd been buried in the first slide was now under six feet of avalanche trash that would have ground Robert and me to pulp had we still been there.

My knees suddenly turned wobbly. I sat down in the snow and lit my pipe. Clamping a pipe-stem between my teeth would help to keep them from clattering so loud, I hoped. And I sure needed a smoke. The whole performance hadn't bothered Robert at all. He wasn't even breathing hard from the action. I knew he would never stop laughing at me if he happened to realize I'd been spooked.

But he was paying to attention to me. There was a half grin on his face as he looked at the piled up snow and all the debris.

"Damn it, Wyman, we lost the shovel."

"Y---h," I said.

It's fun to look in my box of memories now and then.

Some still shine and sparkle.

Editor's Note: Robert Salfisberg was killed along with Chris Kness in a snow avalanche between Midway and the Terry Tunnel in February, 1927.

Here are the men at work clearing the tracks in Animas Canyon. Jim Bell Photo/Gerald Glanville Collection.

Heading down the tracks. John McNamara Collection.

Rapid Transit

Travel in the winter time has its disadvantages and its pitfalls. In any event, it is an adventure—often exciting with a little fun mixed in.

The last winter the Gold King Mill at Gladstone was in operation, tractors with snow plows to keep the roads open were still locked away in the future. The only link the little mining camp had with the outside world was The Silverton, Gladstone & Northerly Railroad. Now and then, if conditions permitted, freighters would break a trail through for sleds and haul in a few supplies. But for the most part, we were pretty much isolated.

Getting back and forth to town was a problem, especially for several of us young fellows who liked to take in the dances or have a night out on the town. Trains came up from Silverton only when there were enough cars loaded to justify the trip. Riding in a boxcar loaded with milled ore was anything but plush accommodation. If the weather happened to be good, we'd ride out on top of the cars and wile away the time ribbing the engineer and fireman. We gave them some good advice on how to run a train, offering to show them where the bridges were so they wouldn't fall in the creek with their little engine and put the boiler fire out. The engine crew was not without its defenses. There was a tender-tank full of cold water, and the fireman had no scruples about wasting it hosing down a bunch of wise guys perched up on a boxcar. Everybody had a good time on one of those trips.

Word came one day that there was to be a big dance in Silverton. Four of us decided to take it in and spend the night in town and then come back next day on the train if there was one. None of us relished the eight-mile hike down the canyon. But it was either that, or stay in Gladstone playing penny-ante poker or cribbage and miss all the fun.

Barney came up with a clincher to solve our problem. Why not knock a light handcar together and just coast down the railroad track to town? The track had a fairly steep grade all the way, and with a little help by pushing now and then, he thought we'd make it all right.

Around a big mine or mill, there's always a supply of old wheels and junk that can be put to good use with a bit of ingenuity. In a short time, we had a small handcar all assembled and ready to go. It was a makeshift rig for sure, with pipe axles and tram-bucket wheels. But it fit the track, and we were ready to shove off.

The weather had been kind to us for a few days, cold and quiet, with little or no wind. There was not a bit of drift snow on the tracks anywhere. Hard banks of frozen snow four to six feet high thrown up on either side of the track by the engine snow plows made a perfect roller coaster right into town.

Barney offered to bet even money, or the price of a dance ticket, that we'd be in Silverton in thirty minutes. It sounded like a good bet to Eddie and me, so we called it. Oscar backed off and said he'd keep time for the trip, and set our hour of departure at 5 p.m. sharp.

At first, the car was sluggish. The rough pipe axles didn't fit the wheels too well. We were kept busy passing an oil can back and forth, squirting oil into the journals, while all four of us knelt on the car with one knee and pushed it along with the other foot, like a bunch of kids in a little red wagon.

But when we came to the steeper grades below the Henrietta Switch, our handcar really came to life and took off. Its speed increased until it was literally hurtling down the icy trough, wheels screaming as their flanges strained against the rails. We began to get excited, laughing and pouring oil on the axles while the speed kept building. Eddie tried to use his brake-stick on a wheel to slow us down a bit. It had no effect at all. Barney was out to win his bet, and a slow-down was the last thing he wanted. He took the brake-stick from Eddie's hand and deliberately threw it away. It was the only one we had.

From then on, we had no control over the car at all. Barney had made sure he'd win—that is, if we stayed on the track. Things were getting a little wild.

Somebody started to sing the old railroad ballad, "Casey Jones mounted to the cab with his orders in his hand." That really set us off. I don't think we'd have used a brake-stick if we'd had one. All of us had gone silly with the speed and excitement and came roaring out of the canyon north of Silverton like a bunch of locos.

Then I began to wonder how to stop the thing. Maybe we'd have to jump. Time had run out: We were inside the town limits and still running full speed. At the north end of town where the tracks cross the main street, some teamster had covered the bare rails with snow so his team could pull a loaded sled across. We hit that frozen snow head-on, and our handcar disintegrated. It was wiped out right from under us. We went tumbling and sliding on down the track on our bellies, backs, or however we happened to land. It seemed to me I'd never stop. The snow on either side of the rails and in between them was as smooth and icy-slick as a skating pond.

Finally, I stopped sliding and stood up for a look around. Barney lay flat on his back, arms and legs spread out. It looked as though he might be knocked out. Eddie was up on his hands and knees, slowly getting to his feet. Oscar, for some reason, hadn't slid as far as the rest of us and came limping down the track to see if we needed help.

"Please, Oscar," Barney pleaded, "Look at your watch and tell me what time it is!" His voice sounded as if he was about to die.

"Well, I'm a son of a gun! It's only twelve minutes after five. We made it in twelve minutes flat, Barney." He held up his watch for us to see.

Barney shouted with glee. "I win!" he yelled. "You guys buy me a ticket to the dance tonight."

"Get up, Barney, you bum," Eddie growled. "You're not hurt."

After we'd looked each other over to assess the damage and could find nothing of importance, we went back to see what had happened to the car. The deck and frame were nothing but kindling-wood and twisted pipe. We never did find the wheels. They were buried out in the snow someplace.

The expedition had worked out fine. We were in town with a big evening ahead of us. True, we'd lost our car, and maybe the train wouldn't run next day, and we'd have to hike back to Gladstone in the morning. But Oscar said it for all of us when he said, "I'm going to have a hell of a good time in town first."

The Long Boards

Judging by the performance of today's skiers, I know I never learned to ski—though I spent many weary hours with slats strapped to my feet. Equipment we used then had a great deal to do with it.

The marvelous feats and precisional efforts of today's amateurs would have been impossible on the crude boards turned out by our local carpenter shops. The old planing mill had a more or less standard model they built and sold for a few dollars a pair. The design took advantage of the lumber supply, resulting in a product that was a real implement of torture.

They were usually made from three-quarter inch fir or pine, ten to twelve feet long. The idea was that a long ski would hold a man up better in soft or loose snow. But the trouble with them was, they were so limber they bent in the middle with the skier's weight. So he went shuffling along, both ends of the skis sticking out of the snow resembling a couple of king-size barrel staves fastened to his feet.

You had to be careful not to slide into a depression that would force them to bend beyond their limit. If that happened, they'd snap in two at the stirrups—ski bindings as we know them today hadn't put in an appearance yet. Alone and miles from town or camp with a pair of broken skis, you were in real trouble.

Those old boards had other annoying characteristics too. Invariably, after a fall they'd come loose and glide away downhill, leaving you stranded, never stopping as long as they could find a little slope to slide down. Another stunt they liked to pull was to hunt out the only tree or rock sticking up out of the snow and break their tips against it. I often wished skis were made of flesh and blood, so a broken tip would hurt like hell.

Another trait they had was just plain stubbornness, due in large part to their length. Before starting off, you aimed them in the general direction of your destination, hoping the aim was true. Riding twelve-foot slats down a slope and at the same time trying to control them was just out of the question. You went where they took you. That is, if you could stay with them and didn't lose part of your pants on a small pine tree or bush that was bigger than you thought and shouldn't have straddled. Running through timber, those skis could literally hang a skier out on a limb or bury him under a pine tree, head down, wood up.

Then there was the problem of sticking snow. Candle paraffin or tallow applied with a hot flatiron was the going technique. It didn't keep the skis from sticking very

111

long, and twelve-foot boards picking up a load of snow with each step, were more like anchors than skis. You staggered along, rapping them at every stride with a ski pole to knock the snow free. A few miles of that kind of going, and you were a candidate for "Timberline Insanity."

A long ski pole, an inch and a half in diameter and seven to eight feet long, usually without fittings of any kind was essential to a skier riding a pair of long boards. You carried the pole horizontally, gripping it in the middle with both hands as a balance to catch yourself in case of a misstep. Or it could be thrust into the snow on either side to keep from sliding sideways on a steep hillside. But its most important use was serving as a brake while traveling through timber, brush or rough country. You simply straddled the pole and rode it, much as a kid rides his stick hobbyhorse, controlling the speed by the amount of your weight used on the end dragging through the snow between your skis. With a little skill in the use of the stick it was possible to come down off a mountain, through the timber or out of a steep gulch quite safely—well, if you didn't break your neck riding the stick.

Jim Bell's skiing buddies, 1929-1930. Jim Bell Photo/Gerald Glanville Collection.

Wings on the Mountain

From high on the southeast slope of Whiskey Pass and out across frozen Lake Emma is a toboggan run that is fabulous. By February there is snow eight to ten feet deep on the ground. The surface of the snow from the pass to the lake is smooth, cold, and as unmarred as a new tile. To those who love the leap and glide of a flatbottomed toboggan this slope is one of the best. The first downward plunge is almost vertical. Then it eases to a long, steep sweep out onto the lake ice. For a tobogganer, it's sheer ecstasy.

The winter of 1920-21 most of the boys were home again and working at the Sunnyside Mine. They'd spent a couple of years making the world safe by chasing the Kaiser and his goose-stepping pals around Europe. And they left the place in quite a mess.

If you break up the furniture in a joint, you pay the damages. It's an old American custom—any barkeeper will tell you. So everybody was busy digging for raw material to rebuild Europe, now that they'd made the world safe for Democracy again.

Compared to soldiering through a war for Uncle Sam, the Sunnyside mine was a dull place indeed. The rattling of an air drill and the explosions when the round was spit at the end of the shift lacked the excitement the men were used to. Even the poker games and the pin-up girls nailed on the bunkhouse walls didn't help much.

To try to put a little fun and action into their life of hibernation, some of the fellows built a toboggan at the mine carpenter shop. On moonlit nights or after shift in the evening, they'd haul it as high up the Whiskey Pass slope as their courage would permit, then point the thing at the frozen lake and let 'er go.

Those watching from the bunkhouse windows were often treated to some hilarious entertainment when the intrepid tobogganers piled up in a snowdrift and had to dig themselves out.

With the right snow conditions and enough speed, a toboggan will start porpoising. As the speed increases the leaps become higher and longer until the toboggan and the riders end up half buried in a snowbank. No matter if the snow is soft and fluffy or firm and settled, a toboggan is the wildest most uncontrollable thing a man can ride.

There's always a dreamer, inventor or experimenter among a bunch of young fellows. This particular genius and wonder worker had spent his time in the army pulling airplanes out of mud holes and pasting fabric over bulletholes in their wings. He suggested they add a pair of wings to the outfit. No doubt if they put wings on the toboggan, just large enough to make it glide over soft snow at high speed, the tendency to porpoise would be eliminated to a large extent.

The trouble was, by the time they had the machine ready to try out, the snow had started to crust because of warm days and cold nights of early spring. The boys figured this would only make for more speed and a longer ride. However, for the first run they decided not to go as high as usual, just in case the contraption needed a few adjustments.

The thing came down the slope from the pass like a striking falcon until it reached a critical speed. Then it shot into the air and turned a backward flip-flop throwing pieces and men in all directions. The first run was also the last one.

Miners who were watching from the bunkhouse windows hurriedly organized a rescue party and brought the victims into the mine infirmary. Every one of them had a broken bone some place in his anatomy. They were kidded and laughed at by the whole crew, and had to be splinted, bandaged and wrapped in blankets and then shipped down off the mountain to the hospital in town.

That was probably the first flight of an aircraft in the San Juan Mountains. The results were conclusive, and the mine management dried up the supply of raw material for further experiments. They seemed more interested in what was under the ground than what might fly over the top of it.

The buildings of the Sunnyside Mine stand beside Lake Emma, probably in the fall of 1919. Louis Quarnstrom Collection, San Juan County Historical Society.

They're Gone Now

They tore the old Opera House down after all the road show people went to Hollywood to make movies and get rich. The old building and the shows had outlived their time.

The Opera House stood facing Greene Street on the west side, next to the new Miner's Union Hall. Some wit said it had more patches than a hardrocker's shirt. Whether they built it for a store building or an opera house was questionable. It didn't look much like either but was always referred to as the "Opera House".

Accommodations inside were in keeping with the general motif. There were rows of iron frame chairs with plain wooden seats and backs. Two narrow balconies supported by round steel rods from above extended along each wall almost to the stage. As a safety measure, a few pipe columns had been added to brace them up from the floor.

The stage was elevated and well-lighted with the new type carbon electric light bulbs, mounted behind tin footlight reflectors. A garish mural painted on the curtain was all but obliterated by advertising and peek holes. The roller mechanism had an annoying habit of sticking part way up or down. Audiences loved to lend their moral support to the heroic efforts of stage hands trying to get the thing working again. A performance at the old opera house was always something of a celebration.

Patrons in the know always preferred seats in the balconies, or the center section on the main floor. Although the balcony railings were sturdy enough to keep the more boisterous spectators from falling onto the heads of those seated below, they didn't prevent bottles from rolling off, or spills from dripping down on some unfortunate customer. There were many demands for satisfaction and offenders willing to oblige. Whether the best show was on the stage or under the balcony was a matter of opinion.

The great and near-great from time to time graced the simple platform. Nor was Silverton without its own artists. What they may have lacked in training, they made up for in natural talent and dedication. If it was opera star, home talent, or road show that held the spotlight front and center, they played to enthusiastic, perfumed, and elegant audiences.

The occasional Wild West Show that came to town during the summer months was pure delight for a kid. The grown-ups seemed to enjoy them, too.

One of those shows, I'll never forget. It was a shootout, which for action and pure Western corn, topped "High Noon, the OK Corral, and the Sundance Kid" all rolled into one. The hero was a saddle tramp who came riding into a poor little cowgirl's life.

116

She was in deep despair. A gang of ruthless outlaws was stealing her cows. Her old papa had gone to his reward, and there was no one to protect her or to defend the home ranch. Our hero vowed his true love, and swore he'd bring the culprits to justice.

The last act opened with a scene at the rustlers' hideout. Six or seven of the gentlemen were seated at a table whiling away the time at poker and whiskey. Suddenly, the little cow girl's hero stepped through the door and confronted them with evidence of their criminal acts. Compared to the renegades' slovenly dress, our knight of the sagebrush was magnificent. He wore the biggest pearl-gray ten gallon hat I'd ever seen. His shirt was pale green, and about his neck, he wore a purple bandanna fastened with a silver hondo. Two beautiful nickel-plated 45's hung low on his hips, their ivory butts arched wide from his thighs like a pair of ram's horns. Below the chaps—resplendent with silver rosettes—protruded Spanish spur rowels that would give any self-respecting broomtail Saint Vitus Dance. His very audacity and boldness held the outlaws immovable for a few seconds. Then all hell roared and crashed on the little stage.

Every actor on the stage had filled his hand with a gun. Several big 45's belching black powder smoke, flame and thunder need lots of room. The Opera House just didn't have it.

Our hero stood with gun blazing in each hand, cutting the renegades down with lightning speed and deadly accuracy. The noise was deafening. I crouched down beside my dad's knees, wrapping both arms about his legs for protection—anything to get away from those terrible guns.

Almost before the last shot was fired, the audience had stampeded out through the doors. The Opera House was so full of black gun powder smoke we couldn't breathe. Out on the street, people milled around, laughing and joking about the shambles that had been created in the last scene on the stage. Most of the lady folks had had enough. Some had passed out and were taken into a dressmaking boutique next door. Little girls were sobbing with fright. Things had gotten out of hand.

After a short time, the Opera House stopped smoking. A gentleman came out to announce that the place had aired out. Would the patrons please return to their seats so the last scene could be presented for their pleasure?

I wanted to see that last horrible battle scene, with the bodies of the outlaws strewn about and blood running everywhere. To have missed it would have been sacrilege. Dad wanted to see it, too, so we went back to our seats-although I never let go of his hand.

They made a few temporary repairs on the curtain and managed to get it up again. What a disappointment! The hero had one arm in a sling, and was back at the home ranch making love to the little cowgirl. He wasn't even wearing his guns.

What a way to end a show! There should have been a hanging, at least.

The town of Gladstone with the Mogul Mill and the Gold King mill in 1906. San Juan County Historical Society.

The Petticoat Battle

The Petticoat Battle was fought on a bright, sunny January afternoon in Gladstone, Colorado. The year was 1922.

The little mining town, which had been sleeping through long years of idleness, suddenly awoke when The Gold King Mining Company revived itself enough to make one last feeble effort to bring the old mine back to life. By the time the mill had been rebuilt and underground workings cleaned out we were well into the first big storms of winter.

It seemed to me the snow would never stop falling that year. Week after week, the storms came howling down from the peaks until the little town was buried under eight feet of snow.

For almost two months, families who occupied company houses had been virtually imprisoned by the deep snow. When the "January thaw" finally came, they dug out of their burrows much the same as groundhogs. Gladstone began to look as though it was an inhabited town.

Even for those days, the going was more than rough. There was no running water piped into any of the small three-room cottages the company rented to its employees. Each family had to carry in what water it needed for domestic purposes. The supply was a single faucet outside an old assay-office building at the north end of Gladstone's one-block street. Also, there was a watering trough there for company stock. It had to be filled each morning, then drained each evening, or it became a solid block of ice by the next day.

With the break in the January weather, the womenfolk took advantage of the warm sunny afternoons to assemble at the water faucet for a bit of visiting while they filled their water pails. It relieved the men of one of their many after-work chores in the evening, and it gave the ladies a little social hour to ease the monotony of life in a snowbound community. In a way, it was like going to town to do the family shopping.

On the afternoon of the battle, there were six or seven women drawing water and visiting as usual. None of us ever learned, or could figure out, just what started the fighting. But suddenly all of them were mixed up in a grand free-for-all fracas. First they started throwing water from the trough, then began swinging at each other with their buckets. The action got rougher and rougher by the minute.

The trouble was, almost all the men who were not on shift were at home or in the bunk house asleep. So the ladies had the street to themselves and were making the most of it. They made more noise banging their buckets and yelling than an Irish shivaree. The language they used would have made a "Libber" blush.

Old "Pegleg" McClosky, a company mule skinner, was the first to notice what was going on. He hurried over from the barn to try and stop the fighting. A bucket bounced off his head. He went down, and the tide of battle rolled right over him. When he managed to get back up on his one good leg, he headed back for the barn as fast as he could go. If he had to, old Peg could do right well on a leg and a half.

Somebody in the bunk house wised up to the circus out on the street. In minutes, every window on the second floor was jammed with cheering spectators. All of them had just tumbled out of bed and were still in their long johns. (I've never known a mill hand or hard rocker to sleep in anything else.)

No one wanted to leave his place at a window long enough to get some clothes on and go see if he could help stop the fighting. No one was willing to brave the snow and a bunch of wild, fighting women in his underwear. As one of the boys said, "If they were using six guns and butcher knives, a guy might take a chance. But with a water bucket or a skillet, those gals never missed."

By that time, the ladies were getting right down to cases in the action at the water trough. All of them had been dunked thoroughly at least once. Some were beginning to lose items of attire. Every such incident brought a shout of approval from the bunk house grandstand. Each of those gallant gentlemen had chosen a dauntless champion to cheer on to victory and possibly win a buck or two for himself on the side.

When the management heard of the trouble, they shut the mill down instantly in order to release the crew. They sent every man charging down on the combatants with instructions to put a stop to the fighting at once.

The men took a dim view of the entertainment their wives were putting on for the bunk house gentry. They moved in on the fracas like well-trained shock troops and took charge of what was theirs by right of title or contract. Regardless of the noisy squalling, each man shouldered his own property and carried her home. It was a wonder some of the women hadn't been seriously hurt in the ruckus.

Gladstone was very quiet after the battle. It was as though the little town had suffered a mortal wound. Neighbors no longer visited in the evenings. The bunk house bunch were very careful about voicing an opinion. If anyone had a notion as to why it happened, he kept it strictly to himself. The ladies no longer met at the faucet to draw water. What had been a happy little community became a hate-ridden camp.

A few weeks later, the company quit, cashed in its chips and shut the Gold King Mine down for good. Some families elected to remain in Gladstone until a suitable means of transportation could be arranged. But most of them joined the mine crew in a weary trek down country. They carried bedrolls and what personal belongings they could on their backs. None of them had snowshoes or skis, but they fought their way through eight and a half miles of deep snow to Silverton.

The trail they left behind was a shambles, littered with abandoned bedrolls, suitcases, boxes, and sacks of personal effects. As exhaustion weakened them, they threw their possessions down in the snow and struggled on. Somehow, they all made it to town. But it was weeks before the last bundle or sack was retrieved from the canyon, and the icy aloofness so characteristic of winter time in the Colorado High Country closed in. Always the vast stillness returns.

The Petticoat Battle along with the company's failure wrote the finale for Gladstone. Another colorful mining camp of the San Juan had started its slow slide into history.

We Hung Our Lamps on a Portal Post

Dusty could sense something had gone wrong. Nobody hung around the pool hall in the evenings any more. Fred didn't talk to him good-naturedly as he used to. He paid no attention when Dusty begged for a ride. The team went about town to company houses, collecting household furnishings, hauling load after load to the warehouse for storage. The activity confused Dusty. He couldn't understand what was happening. No one had any time for him.

Hard times had come to San Juan County, more particularly to the mining camp at Eureka. The industrial machine Uncle Sam had built to supply allied armies of World War I was grinding down to peacetime level. The Sunnyside Mining Company had notified its employees that the mine would close.

Low market prices for the lead and zinc that the mine produced was given as the official reason for the shutdown. No doubt this was partly true, but in retrospect, I think that through the years company personnel had grown old and tired. They had worked the mine to the end of its planned development. The company seemed to lack competent young men with the drive to inaugurate a new development program and carry it through.

As usual, the early fall days were filled with sunshine. But they didn't dispel the gloom that had settled over town. The sparkle and zest to life had faded. Since Eureka was totally company-owned, it meant everyone in town would have to pack up and leave.

The day and hour for the shut-down arrived. I was working the graveyard shift. At tally that morning, each mill man was to shut down that part of the plant he operated, starting at the top floor with the ball mill section, and working down from floor to floor until every machine stood idle and silent.

About 7 a.m., I could hear the ball mills grinding out empty. Their roar rose to a deafening crescendo. Then suddenly they were quiet. Then the tube mills on the next floor below took up the dying refrain, the tempo of their chorus rising slowly. Those of us with ears trained to listen to the songs machines sing knew they were grinding out dry. They too fell silent. Only the subdued beat of air compressors and flotation machines remained of what was once the mighty voice of the mill.

Editors Note: Dusty was a dog and was the main character of another Wyman book by that title. He was well known to all the inhabitants of Eureka. This story is taken from that book.

The Sunnyside Mill at Eureka around 1932. Every building you see in these pictures is gone now. Zeke Zanoni Collection.

This picture is taken looking down the side of the Sunnyside Mill in the early twenties. A.B. Marquand was the construction engineer for this project. A.B. Marquand Collection, San Juan County Historical Society.

Waiting for my turn, I walked out to my station on the operator's deck. Chris Rosenstock, my shift boss, came slowly from the floors above, checking each machine from long years of habit as he moved along. I caught his glance; he nodded. Turning to the master switch panel, I opened the switch for that floor, then for the two floors below. The silence struck with almost the force of a shock. There was no sound left in that vast plant, except water trickling in a drainage launder. I felt as though I'd killed something; in a way, I had.

I said nothing to Chris. I wasn't sure I could control my voice. I just picked up my lunch box and walked out into the bright September sunshine. Fifteen years with the company ended when I pulled that last circuit-breaker.

Dusty met me as I walked along the warehouse dock. He seemed lost and uneasy. All his life the sound of an ore mill, grinding hard rock, hammered constantly in his ears. He couldn't understand the silence. I stopped for a minute to scratch his ears and visit with him. His soft whine, plain as a spoken word, asked to be assured that everything was all right. He kept turning his head and looking, trying to get a fix on something that was the way it should be.

"Oh, come on, Dusty, stop your crying," I said. "You'll get used to it. That's all there is, boy. It's down the hill for all of us."

Before noon, I tossed my bedroll in the old Ford and headed down-country for Silverton. While I looked for another job, I'd tuck my feet under mother's table.

It wasn't too bad for Dusty, either. The Gray family remained in Eureka for a short time until the details of closing the mine and mill buildings were finished. The transformation of Eureka from a busy mining camp to a ghost town was rapid. Dusty must have had a busy time of it, too, trying to find out where everybody had gone. Finally, of course, he had to give it up and accept things as they were.

One clear fall day, I drove up to the old camp, just to see what had happened to it. Eureka had died. Every house was vacant and boarded up, except the manager's home, the Mansion, as everyone called it. The head accountant had moved in and would remain until further notice. The company store reminded me of an old empty milk can. Everywhere I looked along the street, "No Trespassing" signs were tacked on doors and posts.

Perhaps more from habit than anything else, I walked up the deserted street to Mac's Pool Hall. The door opened when I tried the latch, so I stepped inside, sure the place would be as empty as the other old shacks. I could hardly believe my eyes. Old Mac sat in his captain's chair by the stove, as usual. Dusty was stretched out, sleeping on his blanket behind the old man's chair. I'll be damned, I thought. Well, why shouldn't I expect to find them there? I knew those two old devils would never give up.

Quickly, Dusty jumped to his feet and came to greet me with a soft whine of welcome. He stood up, his paws on my chest, while I examined his nose for quills and scratched his ears. Then I went to the bar to select a piece of candy for him, making sure McNamara saw me place the money on his cash register.

"Dusty staying here with you, Mac?"

"No, lad, he's not. But he comes in most every day for company, and I'm glad he does. The Gray family is still here, but they'll be going soon."

"You going to stay here this winter, Mac?"

"No, lad, no. Sure I'll be moving to town in a few days now. I sold out most of the stock. There'll be no business here any more, although the company has agreed to let me stay for a while if I need to. Have ye found a job yet?"

"Nope, not yet, but I'm lookin'. You heard of anything?"

Mac shook his head, no. I said good-bye to a lonely old man, and went quickly out into the bright September day; Dusty came out with me. We stood looking up and down the empty street. Not a thing moved. He pressed his shoulder against my leg. Come on, he was trying to say. The guys have got to be around here some place. Let's go find them.

"No, Dusty, they're gone," I said to him. "They won't be back. Fred put the wagons in the barn, nailed the doors shut and left. He took Dan and Bill down-country to town. This place is dead and all but buried. You're about the only thing around here that moves.

"Remember how you pretended to walk with a limp because Al's mother suffered from arthritis and used a cane? You did it all the time when you brought her up town. Just trying to show the lady how sorry you were. You pulled the same gag when you were hurt or in trouble, hamming it up for a little sympathy. But you couldn't remember which leg to use. In half a block, you'd limp on at least three of 'em.

"Remember those warm summer days when they flushed the fire hydrants? You'd fight that stream of high pressure water until they shut it off. The water knocked you sprawling, but you'd get back on your feet and try it again. Dusty, at times I thought you'd drown yourself, and how the kids laughed at you.

"I often wondered why you didn't like a man dressed in a long overcoat. Why did you scare hell out of poor old Tommy Cain whenever you saw him wearing his? The little fellow would strip out of it, as though the coat was full of ants. That was a bum deal, Dusty. Little Tommy needed that coat in cold weather.

"You damned Casanova, half the pups whelped around town looked like you. I don't suppose you'd admit to having anything to do with such goings on. But it's a fact, and you know it.

"Well, Dusty, we could stop and chin here for a long time, but I've got to go." I opened the door on the old Ford. Before I could get in, Dusty hopped in ahead of me. I took him by the collar and coaxed him out onto the street as gently as I could.

"Come on, old fella, your folks will be coming to town soon."

I got in and started the engine, turning to wave as the car moved away. He stood with his head low, a lonely and forlorn dog. I'd have sworn there were tears in his eyes. Dusty's world had all but come to an end. The children were gone from the street and school playground. The pals he'd rough-housed with had vanished. I know he thought another friend was forsaking him.

Later that fall, and throughout the winter, Dusty and I often met on the streets of Silverton. He had accepted the change from Eureka to Silverton, and seemed happy enough. He liked to have a little tussle with me for old times' sake. I sometimes remembered our first meeting, when he had knocked me flat on my back in the snow, and then offered me his paw by way of apology.

Al told me they were moving to California, looking for a climate that might benefit his mother. Riding all the way to the West Coast in an automobile, with his family, must have been a real payday for Dusty. That's the last I knew of my friend Dusty for many years, and the last of Eureka, the working mining town as I had known it. It made a person sad.

Honky-Tonk Ghosts

hirty-five years of calendars had crumpled up and fallen from the walls since I'd passed that way. Time, fire and cruel winter blizzards had about obliterated Red Mountain Town. The old-timers thought they'd found a silver bonanza, tucked away in this timber-line basin, on the north slope of Red Mountain Divide. So they built their town there.

But the silver ore played out quickly, and their town never amounted to much. The main street was just a little wide stretch of county road. On the west side there was a roadhouse with its outhouses, shanties, and stables where the overland stages nooned and changed teams for their afternoon run. A saloon or two, a few houses and cabins on the east side was as far as Red Mountain Town was able to grow.

I'd parked my car beside the new Colorado Highway number 550 that loops its way in long sweeping hairpin curves up over Red Mountain Divide. Then I walked a half mile or so into the basin; just to see if anything remained of a mining camp where, as a youngster, I'd learned some truths about life in the mines.

From a low rise where the old stage road I followed dipped down into the basin, I had my first glimpse of what was left of the town. A creek had jumped out from behind banks where they'd pushed it to make room for a street and washed a new channel right through town clear to the north end. Probably it was back splashing along in its original bed. Only one building, a roadhouse, had withstood the slow decay of abandonment. Willows and alder bushes crowded in from steep hillsides. Columbines, fireweed, and yellow mountain sunflowers had taken root around tumbled down mortarless, loose rock foundations. The rectangles they formed, all in a row along the east side of the street, looked like flower beds or graves in a cemetery. I was a bit resentful of some woodchucks whistling at me from their lookout rocks. And I mumbled impolite remarks to a pair of blue jays who were making my visit their business. The clamor of the woodchucks and jays jarred. If ever a settlement had become a ghost town, Red Mountain Town was one.

When I turned to retrace my steps to the car, an impulse nudged me to take a closer look at the roadhouse that had been, among other things, the stage depot, a dance hall, and saloon. Since it was still upon its foundations, one last look might be worth while.

Some one had nailed planks across the depot door, but the barroom hadn't been protected with a barricade of any kind. What had once been a board sidewalk had rotted away to a mat of brittle chips and pieces of moldy wood. I pressed the latch down,

The mail sled arrives in Red Mountain town in the 1890's with a couple of good looking ladies besides. Warren Prosser Collection, San Juan County Historical Society.

and the door gave a bit. It was dragging so heavily on the floor boards, that it took a hard shove to get the weathered old panel open enough to squeeze through.

I could have saved myself the trouble. There was nothing left in the barroom. Vandals had stripped it clean. On one wall a great scar marked the place where a back-bar stood. They'd ripped the wetbar out by its roots too, leaving open wounds in the floor. Sunlight streamed through cracks between logs of the outer wall, where wainscoting had been stripped away. I set an old plank bench up on its forked legs, straddled it, and sat down while I looked around trying to remember what the place was like before the vandals and pack rats turned it into a shambles.

The back-bar had been quite elegant, its dark mahogany accenting the mirrors, crystal and cut glass. Deal tables with their green felt tops and heavy varnished chairs sat along the walls; no barroom was ever without them. The floor had somehow escaped most of the destruction, except where its soft pine wood had been worn away from between the hard knots by a small army of hobnailed boots. The knots stuck up like warts on a toad's back. And it seemed to me I could still smell the reek of spilled malt liqueur, powder smoke that perfumed miners' clothes, and the stench of raw ammonia fumes from piles of manure in the stables next door; all of it tramped into the soft wood floor by the tread of heavy boots. And of course there had been an upright piano standing against the back wall.

Surprisingly, by some quirk of fate or chance, the old tune maker was still there, almost buried under a pile of trash. I got up from my bench and kicked some of the rubble aside. Its back casters were gone, and it leaned lazily against the wall for support. The keyboard was a mass of wreckage, keys yellowed, broken and missing. The mountain pack rats must have had a musician among their number; evidence was all over the old music box.

For some reason, I don't know why, I tapped the middle C key with my finger. It was impossible for that battered piece of junk to sound a musical note. But it did! The whole chord for the key of C, both treble and base, came rolling out, clear, loud and tone true. Startled, I stepped back and slumped down on my bench again. The old relic had come to life.

"What the sam hill was going on here?"

Someone was playing the piano, but I couldn't see him. Whoever it was, or whatever it was filled the barroom again with music. The Song of the Forty Niner's was the first selection he played. He followed that with The Old Chisholm Trail, Pretty Red Wing, Sweet Alice, Ben Bolt, Sam Bass, The Settler's Song, Red River Valley and a dozen more. All sandwiched in between the ragtime ramblings of a Honky-Tonk piano-key thumper. The concert ended suddenly. A pack rat that lived in the piano, scurried right between my feet and dived into a hole in the floor.

I yelled and jumped up, flipping the bench upside down. It lay there holding both forked legs straight up in the air, in token of surrender. The barroom had gone silent, so I tapped the C key to get things going again. Nothing happened. I tried several keys, all with the same result. Nothing. That stupid rat had spoiled everything.

The best way to find out what had happened was to look inside the piano. Its harp wires were rusted and broken with hardly a hammer in place. My friend the pack rat had filled most of the space inside with his gatherings. The whole thing was a stinking mess.

I was beginning to understand what had happened. The plank bench still lay with its forked legs raised, begging for help. So I set it up in front of the piano, as a piano bench. It was far too low. Nobody could sit on that thing and play. Only a ghost could do that; they can do anything. I could feel them around me everywhere. My hair started pushing my hat up off of my head. I got the message, closing time. The best thing for me to do was get out of there.

Squeezing through the door again, I pulled it shut letting the latch fall in its keeper. There was no particular reason to fasten it. Spooks can't be shut in or out.

What little breeze was stirring brought fragrance from wild flowers growing along the creek banks and over by those old foundations. A welcome respite from the smell of rotten wood and mustiness of the barroom. An evening sky was darkening so that its stars could shine through. The town's woodchuck sentinels had stopped their piping, and the blue jays had signed off and gone to roost. It wouldn't have surprised me if the creek had stopped its happy splashing, hunkered down in its bed, and started to snore softly.

Old Red Mountain Town was back to sleep again, tired from a hard day. A visitor had come, and now it was time for him to go.

Old Nate's Christmas Party

December 24th that year was a day as clear and cold as a cup of fresh mountain spring water. Perfect weather for my eight mile ski trip to get home for Christmas.

Since I was the only citizen wintering in Gladstone, I couldn't just step onto my skis and take off down the trail for town. There were certain arrangements and duties that had to be attended to.

A supply of dry biscuits was laid out for Pete, a squirrel who lived in a clump of spruce out behind my shack and woke me up most every morning with his chattering demand for breakfast. A few griddlecakes, left over from the day before, were tossed up on a shed roof to keep the camp-robbers (Canadian Jays) in victuals for a day or two. Pete never got wise to their private dining room, so we all lived together on friendly terms, unless Pete caught a Jay stealing a piece of biscuit that he hadn't hidden too well.

A little after noon, I had things all shipshape, the firewood was stacked inside to keep it from getting buried under snow, if it stormed. The water pails were empty to keep them from freezing, and my supplies were stored in a small cellar under the floor, all covered tightly to protect them from frost. Finally, settling the shoulder straps of my packsack comfortably, I kicked my feet into the ski stirrups and slid off down the canyon trail.

An eight mile run down out of that mountain chasm was always a challenge. There is avalanche hazard in every mile of it. A broken ski, or a sudden rise in temperature could mean trouble for a man traveling alone. Only one other person lived in the canyon—Old Nate, a prospector working his claim, about two miles down the trail from my shack.

The skiing that afternoon was perfect, the snow was settled and safe on the steep hillsides and frozen enough to be stiff under my weight. The going was great. Almost before I realized it, I'd covered the two miles to Nate's cabin. At any rate, I was looking up a steep mountain side to where it stood, deep in the snow, about a half mile off from the trail.

Blue wood smoke made a faint plume above his chimney. It told me that the old man was up on his feet and able to care for himself. The years he carried were getting a bit heavy. My afternoon was slipping away and climbing up to Nate's house would take time, make me late, and I'd have to run the last of the canyon at night, by moonlight. But you don't pass up a friend's camp when you're headed out for a holiday, especially on Christmas Eve. The only thing to do was climb up to his house for a short visit.

It took considerable hammering on the door with a ski pole before he heard me and yelled, "Come in."

"Hello, Nate. I'm headed for town. Thought you might be going in too."

"No Sir. There's no one in town I'd want to see. Reckon you'll spend Christmas with your folks?"

"Yea, I'll be glad to spend a few days in town. There's nobody in Gladstone to talk to this winter but snowbirds and squirrels. If you have a letter or message to send, I'll take it in for you."

"Yes, I have a letter written to my niece in California. I'd be obliged if you'd post it for me. Take off your coat, Sir, and rest a spell. The coffee is hot, and we can smoke a Christmas cigar."

Old Nate hailed from Texas. Extending hospitality to a visitor was a way of life. In his younger days he'd followed the trail herds of longhorn cattle up the old Chisholm Trail from Texas to Abilene, Kansas. Then he drifted west into Colorado and became interested in digging for ore. A stranger, meeting him for the first time, couldn't mistake this tall, gaunt, stoop-shouldered giant for anyone but a Texan.

We sat at his table with tin cups of coffee and a box of Havana cigars. A friend living in Cuba sent him a box every fall, straight from Havana. Those cheroots were a pure delight, and I smoked many of them from time to time, while I listened to Nate's views on current politics. The old man never smoked unless there was a friend to share his cigars with him. And if the coffee was a bit stronger than just coffee, so what? It was Christmas Eve.

The tin cups on the table were empty and cold, and our cigars about half smoked. I'd tarried too long. I'd have to finish my trip long after nightfall under a cold winter moon. Nate wiped his longhorn mustache carefully, first on one side then the other. I knew he would have liked to visit all evening. But the only way to get to the end of a winter trail is on skis, not sitting with a mug of coffee and a cigar. When I had my coat buttoned he handed me a white envelope, stamped and beautifully addressed.

"The folks out there will be glad to know I'm well," was all he said.

I had my hand on the door latch and was about to step outside when I noticed a long bench set against a wall next to the door. There were several shallow cardboard trays lined up on it, each filled with bread crumbs, chunks of biscuits, cracked corn and wheat. A large one looked as if it had peanuts and pieces of walnut meats. On the floor a large paper packing case held two or more flakes of alfalfa hay.

I thought—Nate you soft-hearted old fake. You're going to celebrate Christmas with a big party after all. And I thought you'd sit here all day by yourself.

I knew how the party would go. As soon as the sun warmed up the southwest wall where the windows were, Old Nate would spread his goodies along a wide outside window ledge. And before he'd finished, his guests would start to arrive. The Chickadees, Tomtits and little snowbirds would come first, then the Blue Jays, Canadian Jays, and Pine Squirrels. The hay he'd lay out on hard packed snow, in front of the door, for a family of snow shoe rabbits who lived under a great pile of mining timber stacked behind Nate's cabin. I'd bet the old man was planning a party that would last until the sun went down Christmas Day.

He'd move his table up close against a wall under the windows and eat his Christmas dinner there with his friends. He'd slide a window sash back, and the squirrels and jays would hop in and out to share a special tidbit with their host. They were in the habit of doing that whenever they found a window open.

Nate's guests would come to his Christmas party dressed in their best. He would greet the rabbit family wearing snow-white coats and with their ears trimmed with black to match their eyes; the squirrels dressed in reddish brown and gray suits of finest fur, their tails immaculate and fluffed against the cold; and the jays and little birds in capes of feathers and down, exquisite as fairies cloaks. All of them in raiment no king's wardrobe could best. In honor of the occasion, old Nate would have a clean shirt and a tie, as he always did on Sundays and holidays. The Christmas party at Nate's cabin was going to be a grand affair in the true spirit of Christmas.

A moon that I'd counted on to make nighttime traveling easier cleared the eastern skyline, filling the canyon with a silver light. My skis hissed softly as they slipped along. The going was easy and fast. On a night like this, great avalanche tracks held no threat of danger as I crossed them. They were just wide highways up steep mountain sides to the stars. The same stars that lighted another Christmas a long time ago.

Cabins in the mountains, only for the hearty. Jack Stern Collection.

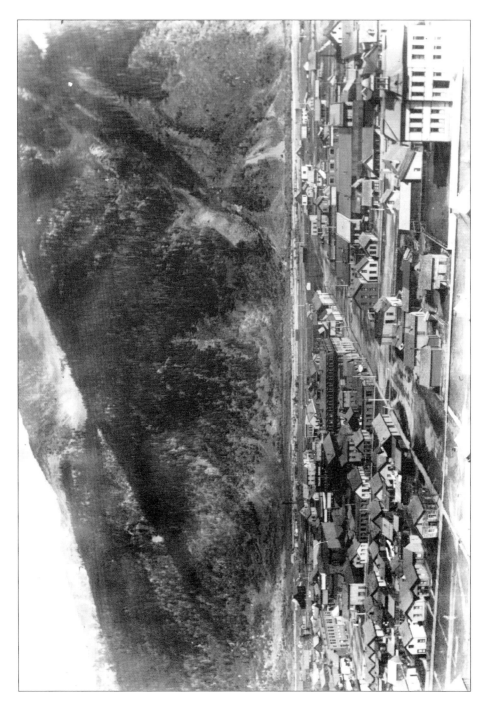

Looking across the town of Silverton towards Swansea Gulch, early 1900. Ray Doud Photo, Jim Bell/Gerald Glanville Collection.

IN MEMORIAM

I have always loved that poem Dylan Thomas wrote to his dying father. It begins:

Do not go gentle into that good night
Old age should burn and rave at close of day;
Rage, rage against the dying of the light.

Rage has always seemed to me the proper emotion to express toward dying. No, no, I won't go. There's so much more to do.

And yet, the gentle going of a good friend, Louis Wyman, one of my favorite students in my South County Senior Center writing class who came for many years until his health prevented it, has made me reconsider my attitude.

He had so many stories left to tell of his life in Colorado mining towns. Stories of humor, of worthwhile humans involved in making life better for others, of pathos untouched by syrupy sentiment. How could he not rage at being deprived of the chance to tell even more stories than he had already published?

Louis had worked as a mechanic but he was a storyteller at heart, one who delighted in telling stories aloud, but also delighted in writing them down. I couldn't teach him much about writing that he didn't instinctively know. Two of his books of reminiscences were published, and many articles and even poems were published by the Silverton Standard newspaper. He was Silverton's unofficial historian. Never the hero of his stories, he only reported what he had witnessed.

Now his voice is silent. He went gently at 89, five years after the death of Elsie, the wife he cherished in life as well as in death.

Written by Ann Saling, Louis' teacher at Edmonds Community College.